SHERLOCK HOLMES

and the BAKER STREET IRREGULARS

CASEBOOK N•. 2

THE MYSTERY of the CONJURED MAN

TRACY MACK & MICHAEL CITRIN

ORCHARD BOOKS
An Imprint of
SCHOLASTIC INC.

New York Toronto London Auckland Sydney
Mexico City New Delhi Hong Kong Buenos Aires

Of the many sources we consulted,
the following were particularly helpful:
The Annotated Sherlock Holmes by Sir Arthur Conan Doyle, edited by
William S. Baring-Gould; *The New Annotated Sherlock Holmes* by Sir Arthur
Conan Doyle, edited by Leslie S. Klinger; *London Characters and Crooks*
by Henry Mayhew; *Frauds, Scams, and Cons*, by Duane Swierczynski;
The Illustrated Police News, edited by Steve Jones; *What Jane Austen Ate
and Charles Dickens Knew* by Daniel Pool; and *The Victorian Underworld*
by Kellow Chesney.

ISBN-13: 978-0-439-83667-8
ISBN-10: 0-439-83667-0

Text copyright © 2009 by Tracy Mack and Michael Citrin

All rights reserved. Published by Orchard Books, an imprint of Scholastic Inc.
ORCHARD BOOKS and design are registered trademarks
of Watts Publishing Group, Ltd., used under license.
SCHOLASTIC and associated logos are trademarks and/or
registered trademarks of Scholastic Inc.

10 9 8 7 6 5 4 3 2 1   09 10 11 12 13
Printed in the U.S.A.   40
First edition, June 2009
Book design by Steve Scott

For Levi Harrison Citrin

"As a rule . . . the more bizarre a thing is the less mysterious it proves to be."

— Sherlock Holmes

"The Red-Headed League"

Esteemed Reader,

Once again, I ask for your patience in allowing me
this small introduction.

If you have read *Casebook No. 1: The Fall
of the Amazing Zalindas*, you now know that
Sherlock Holmes — the world's first and finest
consulting detective — did not work alone. Many
have heard of his friend and biographer, Dr. John
Watson, who took great pride in his contributions
to Holmes's cases. But though Watson was a loyal
companion, he could hardly be considered skilled
in the science of deduction. Still, up until now, he

has taken credit for assisting the master detective and failed to recognize those who helped most.

Holmes's real assistance came from a gang of street urchins who acted as his "eyes and ears" on the street and played a central role in his crime solving. I speak of none other than the Baker Street Irregulars!

These valiant boys have been dismissed by Watson — through ignorance or intention we shall never know — and overlooked by historians. To this day, their efforts remain largely unreported. Don't you agree this omission is a crime in itself? And further, that the time has come to give the Irregulars their due?

I implore you: Share this information with others. For only then may justice prevail.

But I am getting ahead of myself. First, I invite you to travel with me once more to Victorian London, a time when children were robbed of their childhoods, a place where the poor were treated miserably, struggled for basic existence, and rarely rose above their station. Under such conditions, the Baker Street Irregulars suffered gravely. But fortunately, through the ingenuity and survival instincts of their leaders — Ozzie, with his keen mind, and Wiggins, whose street smarts rivaled London's most talented criminals — the gang endured.

Before you set forth into this dark and treacherous world, I must warn you: This story is not for those with fragile constitutions or the weak-minded. What follows involves crooks, thieves, and murderers! But you've read this far, so I trust you are courageous enough to continue. Perhaps you'll even discover a clue to my identity.

Remember this: He who reports the facts must be close to the action.

Now, as Sherlock Holmes said, "You know my methods. Apply them!"

Yours anonymously
London, England
1955

— CHAPTER ONE —

THE CURIOUS DEATH OF GRETA BERLINGER

Rays of green light swirled around Konstantine — a delicate boy of fifteen — as he stroked his crystal ball.

"We gather this evening to seek the spirit of Gunther Berlinger. O spirits, speak to me!" Konstantine's young face was limned with an unearthly radiance. He was fair-skinned with a prominent chin, upturned nose, and curly blond hair. He looked, at first glance, like a cherub. But his voice, which bore the assurance of a worldly adult, and his eyes, fierce black orbs rimmed with indigo, betrayed his angelic appearance.

The parlor was dim. Only the glow from the crystal at the center of a round mahogany table gently illuminated the faces of the five people present.

To Konstantine's right sat his female custodian, Tara, a pointy woman with a bustle of coarse dark hair framing her gaunt face, and to his left, his male custodian, Christopher, a stout, ruddy-faced man whose mouth was set in a firm grimace, like a capsized boat. Between them, Konstantine's guests, Mrs. Greta Berlinger and her niece, Elsa Hoff, leaned forward anxiously in their seats.

The year was 1889, the month November. A chill wind blew in off the River Thames and rattled the windowpanes of the Gothic-style mansion where they met in the London neighborhood of Chelsea.

"O spirits from the hereafter, bring forth the man of whom I speak, for his beloved awaits." Konstantine's voice swelled in strength.

A guitar resting against a floor-length mirror lifted off the ground and began to strum on its own. The tune had a thoughtful, distinctly Bohemian flavor.

Greta was experienced in occult matters and had seen such a phenomenon before. She focused intently on the crystal, her soft, powdered face quivering with anticipation. Elsa looked for strings manipulating the instrument and then fixed her pale green eyes on the boy.

Konstantine hummed and chanted in tune with the guitar's melody. Odd syllables emanated from his mouth. He grunted and howled in voices different from his own. The voices echoed throughout the parlor, as if invisible people were vocalizing all around them.

Gradually, the crystal's glow melted from green into yellow, and then into white. Konstantine's chair levitated three feet off the floor and swung from side to side as he raised his hands.

Elsa narrowed her eyes and stared disbelievingly. Greta watched the boy in awe. She had been to many séances but had never witnessed anything like this, not even on her two prior visits to Konstantine. She squeezed the silk handkerchief in her palm, hoping desperately that, after all these years, she would finally see her husband again.

In an instant, the spinning rays of the crystal ball stopped, gathered together, and shot a single white beam straight up to the ceiling. The guitar quieted and lowered itself. Konstantine's chair settled to the ground.

The young medium drew his palms up to his face. "I have found the spirit you seek! But he comes forward reluctantly, for the dead do not like to be disturbed."

Greta stifled a sob as she dabbed her eyes with her handkerchief.

A moment later, a flash pierced the air. From a cloud of smoke behind Konstantine, an apparition appeared: a man, tall and ruggedly built, wearing a safari suit. He had white hair; a neatly trimmed, push-broom mustache; and dark brown eyes. His form was entirely human, except that he glowed iridescently.

Greta gasped loudly, her eyes enlarged. Elsa recognized her uncle immediately. She drew a quick breath and reached for her aunt's hand.

The apparition motioned lovingly toward Greta. "My little *Bisho*," he whispered.

Greta clutched her chest and screamed. As she fell off her chair, her last word — "Gun" — bled from her mouth in a choked gurgle.

CHAPTER TWO

A GUEST ARRIVES AT THE CASTLE

In London's bustling West End, northeast of the mansion where Greta Berlinger had met her death, a tall, wiry boy named Osgood Manning leaned against a grand but dilapidated carriage. It stood on blocks in the center of an abandoned carriage factory. The space was dank and worn, but to him and the rest of the Baker Street Irregulars who called it home, it was the Castle.

Ozzie held up a stained map of Oxfordshire, torn from an old book. The map was marked with X's, which covered the region in a haphazard design. He studied them purposefully, his deep-set sapphire eyes flickering with hope.

"Each X signifies where I posted a letter to my great-aunt Agatha," Ozzie explained. He was counting on his grandfather's sister to have some information about his father.

Ozzie's best mate, Wiggins, came closer to see. He blew out his cheeks and whistled. "There must be somethin' like twenty marks there. That's a lot of *groat*, Oz."

Ozzie considered his friend. He was half a head shorter than Ozzie but nearly double his girth, with copper curls and kind hazel eyes that shined like new pennies. Normally, Ozzie loved how Wiggins approached every problem with an optimistic yet practical spirit. But now his sound thinking felt to Ozzie like a cold, wet towel.

"I'll never find her by blindly mailing my letter to every town and village in the area. I have to go there myself," he said indignantly.

"But, Oz, what if she's moved on, or dead?"

Ozzie's expression darkened.

Wiggins recognized the faraway look. He knew Ozzie had a sensitive temperament and was prone to fits of brooding whenever anything disturbed his plans. Wiggins clapped a hand on his mate's back. "I didn't mean *to get up your nose*, Oz. If you're *daft* enough to go on this quest, well then . . . I guess I am, too. You need someone to take care of you."

Ozzie shook his head. "I appreciate your concern, but I have only enough money for one traveler. And besides, who would take care of them?" Ozzie motioned with his arm toward the rest of the gang, a motley assortment of boys, between the ages of seven and twelve. Some of them were cooking breakfast over the fire pit while others reclined on the catwalk that ran along the upper perimeter of the Castle. All of them had lost their parents, and they relied on Wiggins for food and work and a place to live together.

Ozzie looked around: A pile of hand-sewn leather moccasins in various sizes sat by the trapdoor. On the wall beside it hung a chore wheel and, on the facing wall, a faded print of Her Majesty Queen Victoria. Alongside the fire pit, one of the boys had scratched out a large rectangle with several smaller ones inside it, denoting rooms: a kitchen, scullery, parlor, and library, which contained a stack of pilfered *Strand* magazines. Other found or stolen items dotted the workshop area: thin pillows, moth-eaten wool blankets, decks of cards, writing tablets, a chipped teapot, horseshoes, and a pair of handcuffs.

The Castle had indeed become a home to Ozzie during the past few months. And he was grateful to be freed from his apprenticeship at the scrivener's shop and to have a place where he belonged. But he had to at least *try* to find Great-aunt Agatha. She was the only person who might know the whereabouts of his father.

Sure, Ozzie never had as good a friend as Wiggins. And he'd grown fond of the rest of the Irregulars, too (most of them, anyway). It was terribly exciting working for the world-famous consulting detective, Mr. Sherlock Holmes, too. Still, nothing could compare with finally meeting his father.

Just then, a scratching sound coming from the trapdoor snapped Ozzie from his reverie. The other boys looked on anxiously as the door swung open, revealing the head of a huge animal that looked half dog, half lion.

"There you go, boy. Welcome 'ome. Come on now, don't be shy."

The dog lumbered reluctantly into the Castle. Alfie, the youngest of the Irregulars, strained his skinny frame against its rope lead.

"What are you doing, Elf?" Wiggins yelled as boy and beast approached.

Alfie may have been the smallest lad in the group, but he always concocted the biggest schemes, and possessed the biggest ears, too, which had earned him his nickname.

"Take that filthy creature out of 'ere." Wiggins pointed to the trapdoor.

"This 'ere is King 'Enry, and 'e's a blood'ound," Alfie said, trying to keep the dog from jumping on Wiggins. It had a thick black coat that was wet and matted, a broad head, deep-set eyes, and jaws that were frothy with saliva.

"If he's a blood'ound, then I am the bloody Prince of Wales." Elliot laughed and plunged his cooking stick back into the fire. He was a bear of a boy with flaming red hair and a fiery temperament to match. The boys sometimes called him "Stitch," because of his talents as a tailor. And for the scars he'd left on many a ruffian who'd tried to mess with the gang, too. Every part of him — his hard eyes, his downturned lips, even his orange freckles — seemed to seethe with anger.

Ozzie tried to find it in his heart to forgive Elliot's prickly nature. A house fire had claimed his whole family, including his beloved baby sister, Maureen. Elliot still woke in a sweat some nights, calling out for her. Ozzie could relate to that. His own mother had died less than six months ago. He could still hear her voice in his head, reminding him to drink the cod-liver oil for his weak lungs, or encouraging him to read as much as he could, or telling him proudly that he would one day rise above her station as a hotel maid and do important work. Still, Ozzie thought, as he watched Elliot glare at Alfie and the giant dog, he was a har bloke to warm up to.

"I must say, I can smell 'im from 'ere." R

smiled down from the catwalk where he sat stroking Wiggins's pet ferret, Shirley. Though he was born in London, his parents — both dead now — had been from Calcutta. But where Elliot was haunted, Rohan was even-tempered and quiet and modest. He was also as strong as he was tall, and the boys counted on him to rescue them from the most dangerous situations. Unlike Elliot, he didn't like to use his brawn. Seeing anyone in pain — even the stray dogs that prowled London's alleys — made him sick.

"King 'Enry's a special kind of dog, a rare beast he is, and smart besides." Alfie pulled the dog farther into the room. "Look 'ere. 'Enry sit, sit 'Enry."

To the Irregulars' surprise, the dog promptly obeyed. Alfie beamed, placed the rope on the floor, and patted King Henry's head, which was higher than his own.

"You see, he's trained and all. He's a real lood'ound and can 'elp us solve cases." Alfie atched King Henry behind the ears. "I found lown by the river. They say he used to belong

12

to an old mudlarker who drowned. I 'eard tell that King 'Enry once dug up buried treasure in the river for the old fella." Alfie's large ears very nearly flapped with pride. His white-blond hair seemed to sparkle in the dim lamplight.

"How would a 'larker have come to own such an impressive hound?" Ozzie asked skeptically.

Alfie shrugged. King Henry gazed at his new master and licked his cheek.

"Does he do anything more than sit?" Elliot asked, removing the cooking stick from the fire to check his two sausages.

"Sure. He knows all kinds of tricks. 'Enry, lay down."

King Henry stretched out on the dirt floor.

Elliot sat down a few paces from the fire, holding his steaming bangers aloft, and nodded his approval.

At that, King Henry lifted his head from the floor, growled and barked. With the speed of a much smaller breed, he sprang up, galloped over Elliot, and leapt on top of him, knocking the flat on his back. The other boys froze.

" 'Elp, the beast 'as got me, 'elllllppp!"

King Henry paid no mind to Elliot's screams, focusing instead on the sausages that now lay on the floor beside Elliot's outstretched hand. With a light pant, the dog picked up the cooking stick and trotted off. He whipped his head side to side until the stick had been relieved of its meat, which he devoured in a matter of seconds. His long pink tongue, speckled with brown patches, licked his jowls.

The Castle rang with the Irregulars' peals of laughter.

King Henry decided to explore.

As the dog gamboled around the fire pit, Alfie caught the lead and bounced along the floor behind him. Fletcher and Pete jumped out of their path as Wiggins gave chase.

Ozzie surveyed the Castle, grabbed Simpson's cooking stick, and held it out toward King Henry.

The dog slowed, trotted over to Ozzie, and rubbed against him in a friendly way. Ozzie offered the ᵃages, which King Henry snatched enthusiasti-before plopping back down on the floor.

Ozzie's chuckles turned into coughs that nearly bent him in half. He staggered back to the carriage and fumbled around inside until he found his cod-liver oil. He took a swig from the bottle and slowly his lungs began to settle.

Wiggins's eyes had followed his friend. At the same time, he walked over to Alfie who lay on the ground, still holding firm to the lead, and lifted him to his feet. Without a word, Wiggins pointed toward the door.

The rest of the boys were either laughing or yelling:

"Elf, you 'ave a prize pup there."

"That ain't no pup, it's a cow!"

"Blood'ound? He's a sausage 'ound more like it."

"Get that *frog a log* out of 'ere!"

Wearing a sheepish expression, Alfie tugged on the rope. King Henry followed obediently as three sharp raps sounded at the trapdoor.

The Irregulars stiffened, ears perked.

Wiggins recognized the signal and nodded Rohan to let in Sherlock Holmes's page.

Billy wore his usual blue wool coa

brass buttons and a matching pillbox hat. Upon seeing King Henry, he inched sideways. "That's some pup."

Alfie and King Henry continued silently out the door.

Billy watched them go, then turned and addressed Wiggins. "Master would like you and Oz to come right away. He has a new client whose aunt dropped dead at a house out in Chelsea — she suspects foul play!"

Ozzie approached from the carriage.

"Who is she?" Wiggins asked.

"Don't know, but she's a beauty! Though she dresses peculiar-like," Billy added.

Wiggins slung an arm up onto Ozzie's shoulder. "Well, mate, looks like you'll have to delay your trip," he said cheerfully. Nothing except food excited Wiggins more than the prospect of a new case. And he couldn't imagine embarking on one without Ozzie.

Ozzie thought for a moment. A mysterious death, utiful lady. It did sound a bit too intriguing to . And while Ozzie wanted to find his father more than anything, it was hard to begin a journey he knew all too well could end in crushing disappointment. "All right then. I suppose I've waited this long."

"Right," Wiggins agreed.

"Let's go," Billy said.

Ozzie strode over to a hook on the wall and popped his bowler on his head. Then with a brief nod to the gang, the three boys slipped out through the trapdoor and into the cold November morning.

CHAPTER THREE

THE TALE
OF ELSA HOFF

A striking woman of nineteen, Elsa Hoff was small and lithe. She had full, naturally crimson lips, wide-set green eyes, and wore her auburn hair cropped. Wiggins thought she looked like some kind of exotic bird he had seen at the London Zoo. So entranced, he realized only after studying her face that Elsa wore the mourning clothing of a wealthy young *man*: gray, striped trousers, tailored white linen shirt, black silk tie, knee-length frock coat, and top boots. He thought she looked sharp.

I'd like to sing a pretty tune for her, he mused. Maybe even ask her for a dance. In his head, crooned:

"It was down by Swansea barracks
One May morning I strayed
A-viewing of the soldier lads
I spied a comely maid,
It was o'er her red and rosy cheeks
The tears did dingle down,
I thought she was some goddess fair,
The lass of Swansea town."

Meanwhile, Ozzie was memorizing Elsa's face. Then he gazed about Sherlock Holmes's well-appointed sitting room. He had been there several times before, but the details still fascinated him: Chemistry beakers were aligned on an oak table; a violin lay across a stack of books on the desk; a Persian slipper filled with tobacco rested on the fireplace mantel; and on the wall above it, the letters *V* and *R* had been rendered in bullet holes! When at last Ozzie's eyes settled on Wiggins, sitting beside him on the velvet settee, he noticed his friend's lips moving silently. He knew Wiggins was singing in his head and gave him a soft elbow to the ribs.

Elsa smiled at the boys and then turned to Sherlock Holmes with a questioning look.

The master detective stood by his desk and casually puffed his pipe. Tall and lean with sharp, intense eyes, and a beaklike nose, he exuded a hawkish fierceness. "There is no need to be concerned, Miss Hoff. These young men are my assistants. They will keep your confidences. Of that you should have complete faith. I do not exaggerate when I say that heads of state have done so in other matters."

Wiggins's chest inflated with pride. Ozzie felt his cheeks glow.

Watson, who sat across from Elsa, grumbled, "I suppose they are of some use now and then."

"I see that you do a bit of public speaking in favor of some cause, suffrage most likely," Holmes observed of Elsa matter-of-factly. "I would appreciate it if you would take the same care in speaking clearly and providing the details of the events that brought you here."

"Mr. Holmes, I have heard about your powers of deduction. In my current state, I am too distraught to question how you have made them just now, though I imagine they have something to do with my attire."

Holmes gave a slight nod of consent, then motioned with a stroke of his arm for Elsa to continue.

Elsa cast her eyes downward and took a deep breath. "As I explained earlier, I have come to see you, Mr. Holmes, regarding the death of my aunt and guardian, Greta Berlinger. Though she was some twenty-six years older than me, my aunt and I were very close, almost like sisters. She gave me everything, Mr. Holmes — education, travel on the Continent, introduction into proper society, and the freedom to live my life in the manner I choose. To the extent I have anything to offer the world, she is responsible." Elsa paused, removed a small handkerchief from her sleeve, and dabbed her eyes quietly.

"My aunt was quite independent and not a traditional woman, but she had a great understandir of societal norms. She raised me in much same way — to respect the mores of our time simultaneously to think for myself." Elsa glanced down at her trousers.

"She was generous not only with me, but with a number of charities and societies. Her one . . . eccentricity . . . involved a preoccupation with the psychical world and Spiritualism. She was an avid reader of the *Light Weekly*, and she regularly sponsored mediums and attended séances. I can assure you, gentlemen, that I have always been skeptical of Aunt Greta's involvement with Spiritualism, and in some cases outraged by it. Most of these so-called agents of the psychical world were outright frauds who took advantage of my aunt financially and emotionally. Still, I cannot deny that I have seen things, on occasion, that were hard to explain."

Ozzie and Wiggins glanced at each other. What sort of things? Ozzie wondered.

"My aunt lost her husband sixteen years ago," Elsa continued. "Uncle Gunther was the love of her ᶠe. He was a dashing man with a reputable charm ᵗ preceded him wherever he went. He wooed my aunt when she was quite young. They were Boers and lived together in the Transvaal, South Africa, on a large ranch."

"How did your uncle die?" asked Holmes.

"The details of his death have never been clear to me. All I know is that he drowned during a hunting trip that my aunt did not attend. A few months after his death, gold was discovered on Aunt Greta's ranch. She made a series of transactions, then sold the ranch to a mining concern, quit South Africa, and relocated to England as a wealthy woman.

"Shortly after her arrival here in London, my aunt and I began to spend time together. Over the years, she took great care in developing my passions: music, theater, and women's suffrage. And when my parents died, she became my guardian. We have no other relations.

"During the past five years, Aunt Greta's interest in Spiritualism grew. As I mentioned, she sponsored a good number of mediums and other mystic types, some of whom she paid tremendou~ amounts of money to help her contact Un~

Gunther. Though a few of the mediums provided some comfort to Aunt Greta, no one ever summoned his spirit."

Here, Elsa paused and stared at Holmes. Ozzie noted a trace of annoyance in her gaze. He turned toward Master, who no longer listened intently, but instead rolled his eyes upward and clicked his tongue.

Watson shot Holmes a disapproving look.

For his part, Wiggins was annoyed with Master for not giving Miss Hoff the courtesy she deserved. She was, after all, a young lady, not much older than himself, and had just suffered a terrible loss.

Ozzie had witnessed Master's impatience on other occasions. It usually came from dislike for the potential client, or dislike of the case. In this instance, it seemed quite plain that Holmes respected Elsa, so clearly the problem rested with the case.

"I assure you, Mr. Holmes," Elsa continued, "that any skepticism you have with regard to mediums is matched by my own. And, as you will see, the world of Spiritualism has had a far more drastic effect on my life than on yours."

Holmes looked Elsa in the eye. "Miss Hoff, I do not doubt for a moment your credibility or integrity. The details you have provided in your narrative thus far are exemplary. Pray, continue." He drew his two forefingers to his lips and waited.

"In the last year, my aunt developed problems with her health, including a weak heart. Her doctors explained that if she did not excite herself, she should be fine. But, in spite of their warnings and my own, she refused to change her life. She continued seeking assistance from mystics. In fact, her failing health gave greater urgency to her quest to contact my uncle. She liked to say it was important to have her affairs in order before she passed on.

"About six months ago, Aunt Greta discovered a young Bavarian medium named Konstantine whose powers were said to be unmatched. Aunt Greta wrote to him and planned a trip to Munich so she could meet him. But the trip was canceled due to a heart attack that left her bedridden for several weeks.

"As providence would have it, Konstantine cam͏ to London two months ago. Aunt Greta and f͏ others, including myself, were invited by him and his custodians, Tara and Christopher Brown, to a séance at their residence.

"When Konstantine first met my aunt, I remember him taking her hand and saying, 'It must be difficult to search for your heart for so long. I can help you.' The boy had presence and as he spoke, he looked at Aunt Greta tenderly, with that angelic face and those unearthly eyes. I thought she was going to faint. The séance itself was like many I'd been to before, but Konstantine clearly impressed my aunt, and afterward she paid him a retainer to secure his services for the future."

Watching Holmes, Ozzie could tell that the master detective was expending much effort to keep his face impassive and hide his disbelief. Ozzie tried to do the same.

"At a second séance, it was only the two of us with Konstantine and his custodians. That time, objects levitated. The boy summoned voices and made ectoplasm appear from nowhere. And he ʰared information regarding my aunt's past that no living person, apart from her, would know. After that, my aunt was fully under Konstantine's spell. Tara, the female custodian, assured us that he would summon the spirit of Uncle Gunther at the next séance. Aunt Greta proceeded to write a bank draft to Konstantine in such a great sum that a large family could have lived comfortably on it for several years." Suddenly, Elsa began to weep.

Wiggins and Watson stood and motioned to offer support, but Elsa wiped her eyes, took a deep breath, and politely waved them off.

"The happenings at the third séance are why I am here." Elsa went on to describe, step-by-step, the entire evening, leading up to and including the appearance of Gunther's ghost and her aunt's death.

As she spoke, Ozzie couldn't help but recall his own mother's voice speaking to him from the dead. His friend Pilar had summoned her. Had it been anyone but Pilar reading for him, Ozzie would have dismissed the incident as some sort of trick. But Pilar was trustworthy — and she and her mother were Gypsies — the powers were in their blood. Ozzie tried to imagine having Mother conjured in material form the way Elsa's uncle was, but the thought unnerved him.

He turned to Wiggins, who was looking down at his lap, avoiding eye contact with Elsa. What was he thinking? Ozzie wondered. Wiggins wasn't always the most discerning investigator, but he could read people better than anyone.

"Miss Hoff, if you will, please describe in detail the apparition that appeared," Holmes said crisply as he strode to the mantel.

Elsa rummaged in her handbag and produced a small envelope from which she pulled a pocket-size photograph. She handed the picture to Holmes. "He looked just like this, except his skin, hair, and mustache were white, as if he had been powdered. Oh, and he glowed."

Holmes examined the photograph. "Did he appear older than this?"

"He looked just as he does in that photograph taken sixteen years ago, frozen in time."

Holmes handed the photograph to Watson. After examining it, he set it down on a small table beside Ozzie, who leaned over to see. The man depicted looked like an adventurer, he thought. His build was athletic, his skin weathered, and his eyes lively. His chin was tipped upward, his mouth slightly open, and he appeared handsome and confident. Still, Ozzie puzzled over a singular detail: He looked as though he'd been caught laughing at a joke he did not understand.

"How did this apparition *dis*appear?" Holmes fixed Elsa with a stare.

"I am not sure. I attended to my aunt at the first instance of her distress, and he was gone before I knew it."

"The word used by the apparition, '*Bisho*,' appears to be some sort of pet name, in an African dialect. Is it familiar to you?" Holmes asked.

Elsa shook her head.

Holmes paced before the mantel. "I do not recall having read about your aunt's death in the newspapers. I find this most surprising, considering the unusual circumstances. At the very least, I would expect to have read of the inquest."

Ozzie noticed that Holmes did not pose the statement as a question. He was directing the conversation — as if the answer he sought simply needed to be confirmed.

Before Elsa could respond, Holmes continued, "You arranged for your aunt to be secretly removed from the scene and then interred in a private burial, avoiding scandal as well as the authorities. That is why you have come to me instead of the police, is it not?" Holmes asked this last question almost sympathetically.

Elsa nodded, restraining tears. "Though my aunt was an unconventional woman, I did not want her death scandalized . . . or her memory tainted."

"You realize that what you did may have violated the law," Holmes said.

Elsa again nodded solemnly.

"Konstantine and his custodians must have demanded a large sum for their silence and assistance." The words exited Ozzie's mouth before he realized he'd spoken them aloud.

"I imagine you are quite right, Osgood," Holmes concurred with a nod.

"Yes," Elsa confessed, wiping her eyes and regaining her composure. She couldn't help but notice that the skinny boy, Osgood, resembled Holmes. "That woman, Tara, was quite coldhearted and seemed to relish the prospect of exposing the situation to the papers. The only things that stopped her were my money and my suggestion that a death on the premises might be bad for business."

"Vultures!" Watson and Wiggins exclaimed at the same time, then looked at each other, dismayed.

"I agree," said Holmes, turning away and crossing the room. "But the real question here is, have Konstantine and company committed a crime?"

— CHAPTER FOUR —

HOLMES CONSIDERS
THE EVIDENCE

The air in the sitting room of 221B Baker Street was heavy with anticipation as the master detective collected his thoughts.

"You understand, Miss Hoff, that I battle only the evil of this world, not the next." He turned to face her from the draperies. "Through my work, I have come in contact with all forms of humanity, but I've yet to become acquainted with a spirit. I do appreciate your thoughtful narrative, and the death of your aunt is indeed tragic. However, I doubt whether a crime has been committed, no matter how disagreeable these people may be." He spun back to watch the street below.

Ozzie felt his face flush with disappointment. The same expression overtook the others.

"Sir . . ." Elsa paused until Holmes turned back to face her. "I confess I cannot rationally explain what I witnessed. But I believe my aunt's fatal heart attack was induced by these people. Will you not dispel the shadows in which these people hide?"

"Holmes, you must!" said Watson.

Holmes dismissed him with a wave of his long arm. "Never fear, Watson. Miss Hoff, I question whether there is anything I can do to bring these scoundrels to justice. And yet, the circumstances surrounding your aunt's death are so unusual, I would be remiss if I did not investigate them further."

For the first time during the interview, Elsa smiled, relief and gratitude claiming equal weight on her lips.

Wiggins clapped quietly.

Watson said, "Good show."

After learning the whereabouts of Konstantine and where to contact Elsa, Holmes indicated with a perfunctory nod that the interview had come to an end.

Elsa stood and offered her hand to Holmes, who accepted it. Watson and the boys rose as well. Watson bowed. Wiggins did the same.

Elsa smiled at him, which caused Wiggins to blush and Watson to frown.

As Elsa was leaving, Holmes raised his left index finger. "I do have one more question, Miss Hoff."

Elsa paused in the doorway.

"Who are the beneficiaries under your aunt's will?"

"I am the sole beneficiary, Mr. Holmes," she answered matter-of-factly.

"Then I do insist, if anything unusual besets you in the coming days, that you contact me immediately."

Elsa nodded in a serious fashion and exited the flat.

Upon her departure, Holmes exhaled a faint sigh. "Watson, my friend, what have I become when I agree to investigate a case where the proposed murderer is dead himself?"

"But, Holmes, you must admit, the circumstances themselves are quite unusual."

"What you see as unusual is merely artifice to me."

Ozzie appreciated Holmes's scientific manner in viewing the mysteries of the world and believed completely in his philosophy. But, like Elsa, he had experienced things that were difficult to explain.

Wiggins, for his part, hoped to get to the bottom of the matter as soon as possible. Miss Hoff was too lovely a lass to carry such a burden, and without a soul in the world to look after her. Though older, she was an orphan like him and the rest of the Irregulars, a rich one, but an orphan nonetheless. He thought of the stories of King Arthur that Ozzie sometimes read aloud to the gang. The quests were a matter of honor, often undertaken for a fine young maiden. Wiggins felt proud and warm at the thought. This case wasn't just work for Master, it was personal-like.

Holmes clapped his hands and spoke sharply, bringing Wiggins to attention. "Though I question the substance of this matter, we have work to d

Boys, I need you to conduct surveillance of Konstantine's residence. It appears to be a respectable address in Chelsea.

"Please note the comings and goings of all visitors and occupants of this building. To the extent you can observe any activity inside, do so, but take no risks. Osgood, as usual, keep notes of all your findings."

"Yes, sir," Ozzie agreed.

Holmes dispersed coins to both boys. "A shilling per day plus expenses for the whole lot, and an extra guinea for the lad who brings me the most significant clue. Remember, survey the scene and report back to me, nothing more." Holmes paused and looked fiercely into Wiggins's and Ozzie's eyes. "No heroics, boys. Our work is to be strictly methodical. For my part, I shall investigate the background of this so-called wonder boy, Konstantine."

Once downstairs on Baker Street, Ozzie asked Wiggins what he thought.

"You know I don't go in for no hocus-pocus," he answered. "Livin' on the streets since I was a youngin', I've seen lots of ugly things, like Master, but it's all been made by people, not spirits."

Ozzie nodded. "You know I am scientific, too, and I follow Master's methods as best I can. But remember how Pilar summoned my mother's voice? That felt quite real."

"You can't explain everything, Oz, but that doesn't mean there are spirits walkin' about, either. At some point you got to decide what you believe."

Ozzie was impressed by Wiggins's assuredness. When he decided on something, that was that. It explained how he had survived for so long by himself.

Turning his mind to the case, Ozzie knew that Holmes's scientific methods must be applied. But if the Irregulars were investigating people who practiced Spiritualism, wouldn't it be helpful to understand their methods as well?

A plan began to form in Ozzie's mind. "Wiggins, you collect the gang and set up the surveillance. I shall go consult with Pilar and Madam Estrella.

Being fortune-tellers, they may have some information that could help us. Who knows, they may know Konstantine himself."

Wiggins gave Ozzie a mock salute before they parted. "Our quest begins."

— CHAPTER FIVE —

MADAM ESTRELLA GIVES OZZIE A LEAD

Covent Garden Market sat in the center of a vast cobblestone piazza bordered by merchant buildings. The grand structure, reminiscent of the Roman Baths, teemed with customers and mongers, hawking vegetables, fruit, and flowers.

"Apples, get your apples 'ere!"

"Roses! Perfumed petals from heaven!"

Ozzie found Pilar by a small fruit stand. She wore an emerald-colored frock a few shades darker than her eyes, a flower-print kerchief over her dark hair, bangles, and dangling earrings. She held up what looked like a stout yellow pear and called in a musical voice, "Quinces, soft, ripe, and sweet!

Quiiiinces! Sweetness from another world, quinces!"
Next to her, an old man with deep rivers carved into his skin stared angrily at each person who passed his stand.

Pilar looked tired, Ozzie noted, or maybe she was just bored.

When she saw Ozzie, her face sparked. She leapt away from the stand and hugged him. "Where have you been?"

Ozzie stiffened as he withstood the embrace, even though he was happy to see Pilar, too. They had met during the case of the Zalindas, in which her assistance had proved essential.

"Master has kept us busy. And I've been planning my trip," he told her.

Pilar crossed her arms and knit her eyebrows. "I have been yelling myself hoarse selling fruit for a wretched old man and going to a horribly boring school in the evenings, while you boys have all the fun."

"Pilar, *¡a trabajo!* Back to work!" yelled the old quince monger.

Pilar ignored him and continued, "Since we quit the circus, Mamá has become very strict. I have been forbidden from conducting readings on the street, which brought in more money than working for this *viejo*. And listen to this: Mamá told me we are not really Gypsies but full-blooded Spaniards. She invented our Romani ancestry to make our act more believable." A stormy look overtook Pilar's face. "She wants me to become a proper *señorita*, and that's why we've settled in London instead of traveling with the Grand Barboza Circus. I don't see how I'll become a lady selling these." Pilar picked up a quince and bit into it. "I still can't believe Mamá lied to me." She could feel a gripping sensation in her chest — anger, indignation, hurt — she wasn't sure which, maybe all three mashed together.

Pilar was *not* a Gypsy? Ozzie thought. What about the reading she'd given him? Was that just a charade?

Pilar read his thoughts. "I *did* contact your mother. It wasn't an act."

Ozzie nodded, feeling unsure.

Pilar could feel his doubt and it stung. "I wouldn't lie to you." Then, pushing the hurt aside, she said, "You have come to see me for a reason. It's a case, isn't it?"

Ozzie nodded again.

Pilar's mood brightened. "Enrique, Mamá is calling," she told the old man. *"Hasta luego.* See you later." Then she took Ozzie by the elbow and led him away from the market.

"Won't you lose your job?" he asked, turning back to see the monger shaking a fist and spewing Spanish curses into the air.

"Ojalá. I wish. But Enrique is a friend of my uncle's and will do anything Mamá says." Pilar shepherded Ozzie out of the large square that surrounded the market and down a narrow street. Ozzie had visited Pilar since she and her mother, Madam Estrella, had left the circus, but he still lost his way on the circuitous streets to her flat.

They turned into an open doorway, where an old woman sat on a chair, swatting flies. Up two flights of stairs, the hallways were laden with the scent of fish, burning oil, and something strong and musky, all of which made Ozzie's stomach queasy.

As they entered the flat, Ozzie braced himself for more smells — orange blossom, jasmine, and frankincense -- and coughed. Pilar gave him a light pat on the back.

The walls and ceilings of the flat were draped in colorful fabrics, the floor covered in a soft carpet. A small round table with a crystal ball at its center stood in the middle of the room, framed by three chairs. Embroidered pillows dotted the floor, and two windows let in a thin light. The kettle boiled on a small stove in the corner.

Madam Estrella emerged from one of the back rooms. She was a tall, striking woman with green feline eyes, silky black hair, and the posture of an aristocrat. Her flowing red caftan with matching head scarf accentuated her exotic appearance. "Pilar, what are you doing here?" Her voice — low and accented — did not sound pleased.

"Ozzie needs our help on a case for Holmes, Mamá."

Ozzie detected a note of contempt in Pilar's voice. He removed his bowler and bowed respectfully to Madam Estrella.

She nodded in greeting, then turned back to her daughter.

"*Hija*, you cannot just abandon Enrique as you please. We rely on him for this flat. Working for him is a form of payment."

"I could make enough money to *pay* for this flat if you'd let me give readings on the street."

Madam Estrella arched an eyebrow. "The matter is closed, Pilar."

"Perhaps for you," Pilar muttered.

Madam Estrella ignored the remark and turned to Ozzie. "*Señor* Manning, you have distracted my daughter from her responsibilities. You are lucky I am fond of you. Please have a seat, and I will pour some tea."

Ozzie looked at the chairs tucked under the table where the crystal ball sat and opted for the pillows in the corner.

Without wasting any time, he recounted the es that Elsa Hoff had described earlier that morning. Madam Estrella and Pilar listened, occasionally interrupting to ask questions. They both considered his words with a gravity he had not expected.

When Ozzie finished, Madam Estrella stood and said, "Poor woman. This Konstantine may have the powers you describe, but he and his custodians clearly lack sensitivity, as well as respect for the living *and* the dead. I agree one must earn money, but there are greater priorities."

"Such as honesty," Pilar offered with mock innocence.

Her mother shot her a look of annoyance.

Ozzie tried to dispel the tension between them with a question. "Have you heard of Konstantine?"

Madam Estrella shook her head. "But nor do I make a practice of keeping current with others in my profession. What I can say is that while there are those of us who can see the spirits, it is quite another matter to summon them in physical form. I have heard of it being done, but I have never witnessed it. If this Konstantine can truly materialize a spirit, he has tremendous powers. But what you have described shows he has poor training and questionable motives."

Ozzie sipped his tea and waited for Madam Estrella to continue.

"I have a friend, Carlos, in Seven Dials, who has traveled far and wide and follows the careers of those with the gift. He is what you'd call a psychical gossip. Perhaps he has heard of this Konstantine and could supply more information."

Ozzie stood, placed his empty teacup and saucer on the table, and thanked Madam Estrella.

Pilar stood as well.

"What are you doing, *hija*?"

"I am going to take Ozzie to Seven Dials," Pilar said casually.

"You will return to Enrique and then attend your lessons."

"Mamá, there are no lessons tonight, and Enrique is set up for the day. Besides, I might be able to help on this case." Pilar paused for dramatic effect. "And you *know* how well Mr. Holmes pays."

Madam Estrella considered her daughter and arched an eyebrow. "You may go, but you will not neglect your responsibilities in the future." She then turned to Ozzie. "Carlos lives in a rough neighborhood, one of the roughest. Both of you, *tengan cuidado*, take care."

Ozzie donned his bowler, and Pilar her cape. Then the two departed before Madam Estrella could change her mind.

Konstantine's mansion loomed through the fog like a huge gothic aberration. "Bloody 'eck, you ever seen such a monstrous building?" Elliot grumbled. It was surrounded by stone walls, fences, and iron gates. The flying buttresses and sharp-pointed arches, along with the stained facade, resembled the manor house of a dreary country village. The building's grim aura stood in complete contrast to its setting in London's quaint neighborhood of Chelsea.

"There's somethin' dark about the place," Rohan agreed with Elliot.

Alfie nudged Wiggins and laughed. "The big blokes 'ave the jitters."

Elliot scowled at him. "You'd be scared, Elf, if you had any sense."

"Enough," Wiggins demanded. The house didn't spook him.

The Irregulars quieted and huddled together on a small side street across from the mansion as Wiggins paced before them. "Okay, mates, Master's orders are to do a thorough surveillance — no one's to come or go without us knowin'. James and Pete, you take the right side of the place; Barnaby and Fletcher, you take the left. Elliot, Rohan, and I will watch the front. On the back side is a tall hedge surrounding what I'm guessin' is a garden. Alfie, you go over there. Shem and Simpson, stay here, remain alert, and be ready to trail whoever leaves."

"Maybe I should go get King 'Enry. He can help us track people," Alfie suggested.

Wiggins leveled a forefinger at him. "To your post, Elf, and no more talk of that mutt."

All the boys took their positions. On the pavement across from the mansion, Wiggins removed his ferret, Shirley, from his coat pocket and stroked her fur. Rohan sat beside them and fed Shirley a few bread crumbs from his pocket. Elliot stretched out on the sidewalk and pretended to sleep. Once or twice before, he had actually dozed off on the job.

"Stay focused, Stitch," Wiggins warned.

Elliot grunted.

A few minutes later, a grand brougham pulled through the gates of the mansion. A well-dressed gentleman in his late fifties stepped down from the carriage and reached up to assist a woman, also poshly attired. A short, brawny man welcomed them at the front door.

The visitors remained in the mansion for approximately one hour. When they reemerged and approached the waiting brougham, they appeared giddy with happiness. Wiggins crept around the corner and signaled Shem who raced around the block, first pursuing the carriage on foot as it drove off, then managing to hop on its rear.

* * *

At the back of the mansion, Alfie was growing weary of staring at the ten-foot-high hedge.

No one can get out through that thing, he thought. Wiggins is punishin' me for bringin' King 'Enry 'ome.

Alfie paced and examined the hedge. That's when he noticed a six-inch break at the bottom of the dense shrubbery. He looked around and, not seeing anyone, dove under it.

He'd been worming through for only a moment when his head smacked a wood fence. He stifled a yelp. Rubbing the spot, Alfie managed to stand and discovered he was now lodged between the hedge and the fence, which stood about a foot taller than he.

"Blimey, I 'ope I'm not stuck," he muttered.

Sidestepping, he at last found a split in the planks and, through it, spied a formal garden. A stone path led through a manicured lawn filled with trees, flowerbeds, bushes, a small fountain, and a few benches. Alfie was studying a stone monolith rising up in the center of a square of paving stones when a man and a woman exited the rear of the house and walked through the garden. The man had black hair with silver winglike patches around the ears, a neatly trimmed mustache, and was dressed in a finely tailored wool suit. The woman was thin as a wafer, with sharp eyes, a pointed nose, and long, wiry hair. She reminded Alfie of a witch.

The woman stopped and said sweetly, "Darling, you *must* do it."

The man shook his head. "But we did not plan it this way." He pulled a white silk handkerchief from his pocket and mopped his brow.

The woman's voice turned suddenly shrill. "Finish this. Finish *her*!"

The man put a hand on her shoulder, seemingly to quiet her. He bowed his head as they continued walking in Alfie's direction.

Alfie watched them carefully, until a cart passing on the street startled him and caused him to glance away.

When he peered through the crack again, the woman was stalking back toward the house. But the man was nowhere to be seen. Where could he have gone?

Then Alfie noticed the handkerchief lying on the ground. He tried to climb over the fence, but landed repeatedly on his bottom. Should he fetch one of the older boys?

Studying the spot where the wood slats met the dirt, he dropped to his knees, heart thumping, and dug like a mole.

CHAPTER SEVEN

IN SEARCH OF CARLOS

The streets of Seven Dials were a frothing cauldron of filth, crime, and lawlessness. Ozzie had explored many parts of London since becoming an Irregular, but this had to be one of the worst. Ironically, the area was called the "Holy Land."

Pilar led Ozzie down fetid-smelling streets and alleys bordered by decaying tenements. Men, women, and children slept together on the ground. A light rain penetrated their thin rags. Ozzie knew how uncomfortable it felt to be stared at, and he tried to avert his gaze.

When they arrived at an intersection of seven streets, Pilar paused. "I always forget if the turn is at the second street or the third," she said with some frustration.

An obese lady in a soiled dress approached her. "Pretty cape, dearie. Can I try it?"

Ignoring her, Pilar said, "Let's go this way."

"Let me give them *glad rags* a try, sweet, just for a moment." The lady followed a foot behind.

Pilar looked over her shoulder and said sternly, "Leave us alone."

"That's no way to talk to a lady." Her voice woke a man who had been lying on the street. His forehead boasted an open wound. A hump on his right shoulder rendered him crooked.

When Ozzie turned back, he saw that the man was now limping after them as well.

"Look at his slippers," the man said, referring to Ozzie's leather moccasins. "They'd keep me feet nice and dry on a day like this."

Ozzie shuddered at the sight of the man's feet. They were black and bulging with sores. He knew there were people in London who would forcibly take your clothes; he had just never met anyone who would want his.

The man and the woman hurried to keep pace. By now, a few boys a bit younger than Ozzie and Pilar had joined the chase. They laughed and yelled, "She's a dark one!"

"You see his silly hat?"

Ozzie grabbed Pilar's hand, and they ran down a narrow alley. Soon Ozzie started wheezing.

They could hear the shouts of their pursuers over the surrounding noise. Quickly, they ran down another passageway where several people slept in one bed. Racing past, they turned onto a main street and back into another alley, all the while dodging stones and rubbish that the boys hurled at them.

"Maybe this was a bad idea," Ozzie said, stopping to bend over and catch his breath.

The boys who'd been chasing them approached. The leader was missing half his teeth and looked as though he'd been sleeping on the streets his whole life. He held an old table leg like a cudgel and pointed first to Ozzie's feet, then to Pilar. "The slippers. And you, the cape."

The obese lady and the crooked man, who had caught up to the boys, looked on and laughed.

"I am not giving my cape to anyone!" Pilar countered.

Ozzie could not care less about his moccasins. He knew Elliot could sew him another pair. It was being chased and cornered that bothered him. He was angry with himself for not coming up with a better plan.

Ozzie grabbed Pilar's hand again and gave a slight nod, indicating that they should charge through the pack.

"The queue forms here, does it? What are you all waitin' for, fish 'n' chips?" A man well over six feet tall and the width of two ordinary men spoke up from behind the crowd. He had wavy, damp hair, the color of wet cobblestones, and he puffed a small pipe.

"Carlos!" Pilar exclaimed.

Carlos winked at her as he asked the boy holding the table leg, "What's that for?"

"It's um . . . a . . . um . . . a walkin' stick." The boy backed away, and the rest of the mob dispersed.

Carlos chuckled, turned toward Pilar, and gave a small bow. "Good morning, *princesa*. I see you've met the neighbors."

Moments later, in Carlos's hovel attached to a tenement building, the three sat on stone remnants around a makeshift table. Carlos smelled of incense, tobacco, and something earthy that Ozzie couldn't place. His hands were tattooed with birds and words in some other language. Carlos absentmindedly flipped through an enormous deck of cards as Ozzie told him about Elsa Hoff and asked what he knew of Konstantine and his custodians.

"Tara and Christopher Brown?!" Carlos's eyes grew wide, and he said something in Spanish that made Pilar blush. He stood and paced the tiny courtyard as he ran his large hands through his hair. "May time curse their souls."

Pilar had never heard such a bitter tone in Carlos's voice, and Ozzie noticed that the big man seemed quite agitated.

"How do you know them?" Pilar asked.

"They're originally from London and worked as table turners not too far from here. That was sixteen years ago."

"What is a table turner?" Ozzie asked.

"It means they are fake mediums," Pilar told him.

Ozzie nodded and turned to Carlos. "What can you tell us about them?"

"They are con artists of the worst kind. Tara is as deceitful as they come — practiced at spinning a web of lies." Carlos seemed to disappear into a memory before resurfacing. "She creates enemies from dust." Carlos's voice was streaked with venom and something else.

Was it fear? Ozzie wondered.

"Oh, she can be charming when she desires, but it's all part of her trap. I myself was foolishly drawn in by her manipulations and her penetrating eyes.

"She and her brother, Christopher, developed an act together. They would invite seekers to their home and attempt to contact their dead loved ones. At those gatherings, they gained the trust of their clients, extracted secrets from them, and then used the information to rob or blackmail them." Carlos shook his head in disgust. A shudder rippled through his towering body.

"Tara doesn't have the gift," he continued, "and she relied heavily on others, myself included, to teach her about the world of Spiritualism. Her desires were always for money. Personal gain is one thing, but she also craved power and tried to eliminate the competition. If she heard about other mediums in the area receiving clients, she accused us of stealing from her act, which was not only false but outrageous, considering I'd taught her everything she knew. When I threatened to expose her, she gave me this." Carlos removed the handkerchief from around his neck, revealing a five-inch scar snaking across his throat.

Ozzie's right hand went involuntarily to his neck.

"Tara is not someone to cross," Carlos said with an uncomfortable laugh.

"Are Tara and her brother still practicing?" Pilar asked.

Carlos shook his head. "They took advantage of the wrong old lady, the mother of an inspector at Scotland Yard, and the next I heard they had fled the country. I never saw them again." He rubbed his eyes and spit. "I don't know Konstantine, but if he is involved with the Browns, there is crookery at work. I will try to find out more. Meanwhile, I don't like the idea of you mixing with these people. *Tienen la mala pinta.*"

Ozzie looked quizzically at Pilar.

" 'They carry the stain of bad people,' " she translated.

Carlos nodded gravely, replacing the handkerchief over his scar before leading them back through the teeming alley and depositing them on a street corner just outside of Seven Dials. "I cannot warn you strongly enough," he said looking down at Ozzie and Pilar, "keep your distance from Tara. She is a soulless creature."

CHAPTER EIGHT

PILAR
VANISHES

And he was gone like that ma-gi-sh-un we saw on the street, rabbit and hat, presto, magic. The only thing left was his handkerchief." Alfie was completely covered in damp soil, with small pieces of branches and leaves wound in his hair. His oversized ears were ringed with dirt. He looked as though someone had just dug him up.

Wiggins, Ozzie, and Pilar listened skeptically. The four of them stood on a side street out of view of the mansion.

"Elf, I think the damp air has clogged your little brain, you poor *sprog*. You're imaginin' things. Let's —"

Before Wiggins could finish his thought, Alfie pulled from his soiled trouser pocket a gentleman's handkerchief. "You think this is a dream?"

Pilar smirked. "I guess he's more reliable than you thought."

Alfie beamed. He was beginning to like having Pilar around, even if she was a girl.

Ozzie took the handkerchief and inspected it. Though apparently new, it was extremely soft — made of silk, Ozzie determined. The initials *SZ* were embroidered on one of the corners. Having been apprenticed to a scrivener, he recognized that the initials were sewn in the style of German Fraktur typeface.

"This handkerchief belonged to a wealthy German," Ozzie deduced. He patted Alfie on the head. "Good work, mate. Why don't we take a look in that garden?"

Alfie lit up and promptly led Wiggins, Ozzie, and Pilar to the rear of the mansion. When they reached the hedge, Alfie slithered snakelike under it. Ozzie and Pilar followed with some difficulty.

Once through, they stood next to Alfie, wedged between the hedge and the wood fence that framed the back side of the garden.

As Wiggins tried to squeeze under the hedge, Alfie laughed impishly. "Too many sausages in your gut, boss?"

Wiggins groaned but finally pulled himself through.

Pilar motioned for them to be quiet.

Ozzie had no difficulty seeing over the fence. Pilar stood on tiptoe, as did Wiggins who lifted Alfie onto his shoulders. A foggy mist kept them well hidden.

"Where did you last see him?" Ozzie whispered.

Alfie pointed to the monolith. "I found the hankie on the stones."

Wiggins knew that Master wanted him to report his findings, nothing more. But the thought of a quest on Elsa's behalf, not to mention the extra guinea and the feast he could cook up for the gang if he brought back the most significant clue, propelled him forward. "Elf, you stay here and keep watch while we take a look."

Alfie groaned with disappointment. "But I'm the one —"

"Quiet," Wiggins instructed before following Ozzie and Pilar over the fence.

Inside the garden, Ozzie paced and stared at the cut stones while Wiggins and Pilar examined the monolith: a four-sided marble column with cornices and flourishes. The top came to a single point about twenty feet in the air. Ozzie thought it was a strange design for a city garden.

"What are we looking for?" Pilar asked. She and Wiggins stood beside the monolith, inspecting its details.

Ozzie continued studying the slate squares beneath it. "I don't believe people just disappear," he said. "There's no visible way out of the garden, so if Alfie saw what he says he saw, there's a hidden passage here somewhere." He traced his foot along the edges of the stones.

Wiggins ran his fingers along the trim of the monolith. In an instant, a piece of what looked like solid marble moved. Pilar gasped. When Wiggins turned, she was gone.

"Oz!" he exclaimed.

Ozzie looked up and saw Wiggins standing openmouthed next to . . . no one at all. "Where's Pilar?"

"She was standing right here next to me." Wiggins indicated the paving stone that abutted the monolith, then pointed to a piece of trim. "Look, there's a lever!"

Ozzie stepped onto the same slate. "Quick! Do exactly what you did before."

Wiggins pulled the lever. Before he could reach for Ozzie, his friend disappeared — as if the ground had opened up and swallowed him.

Ozzie felt himself falling through the darkness. The damp air chilled him. The hard landing jarred his jaw. When he looked around, he saw Pilar holding a candle stub. "Nice ride, wasn't it?" Her face glowed in the candlelight.

They appeared to be inside some sort of hollow chamber, a cavern with rough brick walls and a dirt floor. Even at a whisper, Pilar's voice echoed.

Ozzie stood, brushed himself off, and took a few tentative steps. He spun back around when a thud and a groan startled him.

Wiggins sat in the very spot where he'd just fallen. A broad grin illuminated his friend's face.

"If we weren't workin', I'd say let's try that again." Wiggins was reaching for Ozzie's outstretched hand when Alfie fell howling through the darkness and landed onto his lap.

CHAPTER NINE

EXPLORING
THE TUNNELS

The cavern felt vast. Even though they'd all fallen the same distance, none of them could determine how deep underground they were, perhaps ten feet, perhaps sixteen.

Pilar held the candle stub, which illuminated the cavern and four tunnels branching off it. She led them into the first tunnel. It dead-ended after about twenty-five paces. Two large metal loops dangled from the back wall. From them hung chains with manacles.

Ozzie examined the cuffs. "It doesn't look as though anyone has been chained up here in a long time."

Wiggins had forgotten about Shirley until he felt her squirming inside his jacket. He reached in to stroke her fur. "Nothin' to be afraid of, girl."

The tunnel was damp. The smell of it reminded Pilar of a crypt.

Ozzie coughed and covered his mouth with his hand to quiet himself.

Alfie was too busy tracing his fingers along the brick walls and scuffing his feet on the dirt floor to worry about who or what they might encounter.

They retraced their steps back to the center cavern and then entered the next tunnel. Fifty paces down, they came to a set of stairs. At the top, Wiggins unlocked a latched door, which opened onto a quiet side street.

The strings of Ozzie's mind played together. "This is how Alfie's handkerchief man left the premises." He tapped his left temple with a long, bony finger, trying to determine why the man might not want to be seen.

The gang backtracked to the center of the cavern one more time and continued down the third tunnel. After just ten paces, it curved sharply and the walls drew closer together. Finally, it grew so narrow that they had to turn sideways. When the ceiling slanted downward, all of them, even Alfie, dropped onto all fours.

"It's bloody tight," Wiggins said with a sigh. "Maybe we should turn back."

Ozzie started to sweat and thought he might retch.

Just then, squealing sounds filled the cavern.

Wiggins felt Shirley squirm in his pocket. "Bloody 'eck, what is it, girl?"

"Maybe it's a spirit!" Alfie said.

"It sounded more animal than human," Pilar countered. "Alfie, give me some space, won't you?"

"What do you mean?"

"I mean you just grazed my ankles with your grubby hands."

"But I'm back here."

Pilar craned her neck around. Alfie was a good three feet behind her. "Then what did I feel?"

The squealing sound came again, and this time, Shirley practically leapt out of Wiggins's pocket.

"Whatever it is, it's givin' Shirley the *collywobbles*," he said.

Pilar sat back on her heels, held up the candle stub, and made a full circle, searching for the source of the sound. When she glanced down at the ground, she screamed.

Darting in and out of the holes in the floor were rats. Dozens of them! And now they were scurrying around the gang, climbing up and over them.

Pilar screamed again and pulled the hood of her cape over her head.

Wiggins opened his coat, and Shirley jumped out, going after the rodents like a prize rat catcher. Within minutes, they'd dispersed down the tunnel and back into their burrows. Shirley's instincts were so strong that she never turned back, pursuing the last rats until they were out of sight.

"Shirley!" Wiggins called. But she had already disappeared down the long, dark tunnel. He looked at his friends. "I have to go after her."

They followed Wiggins on hands and knees until the tunnel they were in emptied out into a wider, taller one with brick walls. Relieved, they stood, turned left, and walked about thirty paces only to find themselves back in the center cavern.

"That third tunnel simply runs into the fourth," Ozzie noted, breathing easier in the open space. "If we had turned right, we might have arrived at the mansion. Let's retrace our steps."

As they did so, the candle dwindled, and Wiggins called softly, "Shirley, come girl."

But there was still no sign of her.

"We'll find her, mate," Ozzie reassured him. In the dim half-light, he could see Wiggins nod, but it was an unconvincing gesture. Wiggins and Shirley had been together since they were both small. Losing her would be the next worst thing to losing one of the Irregulars, Ozzie realized.

"Don't fret, boss, she's a smart one," Alfie added.

Pilar gave Wiggins's shoulder a squeeze. "She'll find us, more likely."

They continued walking and soon felt the dirt floor turn to stone. Every few steps, Wiggins whispered, "Shirley," but to no avail.

In the distance, an open doorway beckoned. Light emanated from it.

"That must be an entrance to the cellar of the mansion," Ozzie whispered.

Just then, a howling sound came from that direction, followed by the click of paw nails scratching a tiled floor.

Pilar snuffed the candle, and she and the boys waited in the darkness.

In the lighted door frame, two large dogs barked and strained at their leashes. Behind them, a tall figure loomed. It held the dogs with one hand and lifted a lantern with the other. Luckily, the lantern's beam did not reach them.

Without a word, the gang backed up. Ozzie whispered in Alfie's ear, "Go ahead of us through the third tunnel and meet us in the center cavern where we started. Be quick!"

Alfie did as instructed.

The dogs howled again. The click of paw nails grew louder and faster. The dogs had been let loose!

"Run!" Ozzie told Wiggins and Pilar.

The three sped down the passageway. But within seconds, the panting grew louder still. Ozzie's lungs constricted. One coughing fit and they'd surely be mincemeat. He pushed himself forward.

When at last they arrived at the center cavern, Ozzie bent in half and grabbed his knees.

Alfie knelt beside him, as did Wiggins. "Take slow, deep breaths, mate," he told Ozzie.

The dogs were barking fiercely now, but the gang could no longer hear their paws moving toward them.

Ozzie stood up and listened. "They've stopped the chase," he managed.

"You knew that sending Alfie back a different way would confuse them. The mongrels didn't know which scent to follow," Wiggins noted admiringly.

They all felt a wave of relief — until the lantern light stabbed the darkness and a woman's voice, shrill and threatening, pierced the silence. "Intruders shall be mauled!"

Mauled? What kind of person would speak that way? And then Pilar knew. "*She is a soulless creature.*" Carlos's words wrung in her ears.

Pilar grabbed Wiggins's hand, Ozzie grabbed Alfie's, and they ran. Inside the second tunnel, they could hear the dogs following. They climbed the steps. Wiggins fumbled with the door lock as the light bobbed closer. Finally, he unlatched it and led them onto the street. Once they were outside, he motioned for them to crouch behind some rubbish.

Moments later, they heard the door swing open. They peered out to see a tall figure. She positioned two fierce black dogs on either side of her, as though she were about to give the command to attack.

Ozzie realized immediately who she was.

A helmet of long black hair surrounded the woman's drawn face — the kind of hair that suggested an unhealthy constitution, and the kind of face that was marked with bitterness. Her most striking feature was her eyes, a chilling blue that seemed to pulse. A sign of uneasiness, Ozzie thought. In his work for Master, Ozzie had confronted some of London's most dangerous criminals. But something about this woman unnerved him. There was an unsoundness about her and that, coupled with the "soullessness" in her eyes, was an unsettling combination.

"Tara Brown," Pilar mouthed to Ozzie.

He nodded solemnly.

"Watch out for that one," Wiggins whispered.

Ozzie studied the gaunt face that stared wildly down the street in their direction and watched as Tara snapped the dogs' leads and headed the other way.

CHAPTER TEN

THE IRREGULARS REPORT THEIR FINDINGS

Ozzie, Wiggins, Alfie, and Pilar met the others at the surveillance post one street over from the mansion. A chill afternoon wind blew off the river, clearing the fog.

"That's the witch I saw in the garden," Alfie said.

Ozzie nodded. "I don't think she saw us."

"Did you see those beasts?" Wiggins said. "They coulda shredded us."

"King 'Enry could take care of 'em," Alfie suggested.

Wiggins shook his head. "You'll keep that mutt away from 'ere or you'll be spendin' the rest of this case back at the Castle."

When the four reached Elliot, he said, "Where you *layabouts* been? Rohan, Shem, and I are busy workin', while you're dancin' 'round town."

Wiggins shook his head. "Stitch, you are *all mouth and no trousers*. Now give us a report."

The scolding had no effect on Elliot. "You start," he told Shem.

Shem explained how he'd followed the first visitors earlier that morning. "You saw that carriage. It shined like licorice. I tracked the two old *nobs* to the poshest 'ome in Mayfair. It made that place" — Shem motioned to the mansion — "look *poxy*, mighty *poxy*."

Ozzie noted the Mayfair address on his writing tablet.

Simpson gave his report next. "I followed my man along the Thames straight into Westminster. You'll never believe where the carriage stopped — right in Old Palace Yard. The gent stepped out and walked into the House of Lords!"

Ozzie asked Simpson to give his best physical description of the gentleman, which he also recorded in his tablet.

Wiggins paced. "Good job, mates. Those Spiritualists have a *bonny* business. Oz, you and I should go report to Master and —"

"I'm going, too," Pilar interrupted.

"Fine," Wiggins agreed. He knew Pilar could be useful, and Master did not seem to mind her presence.

"Rohan and Elliot, you're in charge 'ere. If there's any big news, send Alfie to find us. Keep your heads down. There's something about all of this that smells bad."

As Wiggins finished his instructions, Fletcher came running from his station in front of the mansion.

"A posh boy just left the mansion and is walkin' this way!"

"Konstantine," Pilar whispered.

"He saw you come runnin' 'ere?" Wiggins groaned.

"Boss, I swear I moved silent and invisible, like the wind." Fletcher crossed his heart.

Wiggins ran his hands through his hair. "Right. We can't be standin' 'round like this. Rohan and

Elliot, take Elf and the 'Wind' 'ere and move down the street. Then loop 'round a few streets back to the mansion. Oz, Pilar, and I will take a look at this medium *bloke*."

After the other four ran off, Ozzie pointed to a cart. "Wiggins, you and Pilar go across there and hide. I'll sit and scrounge."

Wiggins and Pilar paused to argue but there was not enough time. They heard footsteps approaching.

They sped off and Ozzie sat on the curb and held out his hat.

Seconds later, Konstantine stepped around the corner.

Ozzie looked up, eyes wide and pitiable. A slim, fair-skinned blond boy of about fifteen approached. He was dressed in a blue suit with a black silk cape draped over his shoulders. Ozzie had seen his type of gait before on older, wealthy private-school boys: chest thrust forward, chin held high. But something about his gaze — detached and unblinking — felt familiar and unsettling.

"Are you staring at me, urchin?" Konstantine's voice was filled with hubris.

Ozzie manufactured a cough. "Nice day, isn't it? How 'bout some change, mate?" He held up his bowler.

Konstantine took a step back and examined Ozzie as if he were some strange and vile creature. "It is rude to stare," he said.

"No offense." Ozzie extended his hat again. "It's just . . . that suit is posh, mighty posh, mate."

"I am not your mate. And you should not address your betters so directly."

"Betters?" Ozzie restrained a smile. "Nice word that."

Konstantine squared his shoulders and lunged toward Ozzie. "Watch your mouth, urchin, or I will pummel you."

"But don't get your suit dirty, guv." Ozzie smiled. Though he was younger and slighter than Konstantine, he knew he and Wiggins could knock him flat if they had to.

Ozzie offered up the empty hat again. "Where's that posh accent from?"

Suddenly, Konstantine closed his eyes, stretched his arms wide like wings, and tilted his head skyward. He started to hum.

What is he doing? Ozzie wondered.

"Your father is gone and shall never return." Konstantine's voice was deep and rippled. "Your life is worthless. You are doomed to live on the streets until you die. Only then will you meet your father — in the afterworld." Konstantine opened his eyes and stared fiercely, almost madly, at Ozzie.

Ozzie leapt to his feet and swung at him.

But Konstantine dodged the punch and laughed. "Good-bye, you wretched orphan," he said with a twisted smirk. Then he strode haughtily down the street as Ozzie hurled his hat after him.

CHAPTER ELEVEN

A MEETING AT 221B BAKER STREET

Roughly thirty minutes later, back at Holmes's flat, Ozzie, Wiggins, and Pilar found the detective standing before his desk, poring over a pile of newspaper and magazine clippings, written in English and German. Though still a bit flustered from his encounter with Konstantine, Ozzie noticed that the master detective flipped through the German clippings with the same ease he did the ones in English.

Watson looked up momentarily from his paper, rolled his eyes at the threesome, and resumed reading.

Holmes waved them over to where he worked.

"You boys brought in a specialist in Spiritualism, I see." He gave a slight nod of recognition to Pilar and returned to the papers.

Pilar felt flattered that Master recognized her and that he called her an expert. But she wasn't, she thought. After seeing Konstantine, she had a feeling he was a fake, in part because he seemed too confident for someone so young, but she didn't trust her feelings anymore. Would Master dismiss her if he found out about Mamá's lies?

"Though not as exciting as fieldwork," Holmes continued, "some of a detective's most productive time is spent researching his subjects. Not surprisingly, our medium friends have appeared in a few papers. My acquaintances at the public archive were quite diligent in their research."

Holmes picked up one article, which he summarized. "Apparently, our subjects fled Bavaria just before criminal proceedings were brought against them. Authorities suspected them of snaring and defrauding a number of clients, including several elderly people.

"The leader of the family is a gentleman called Spangler Zweig. His wife, Tara; their son, Konstantine; and Tara's brother, Christopher, all play roles in the deception."

Ozzie listened to Master carefully. The fact that the authorities had pursued Konstantine suggested he was a fake. That was comforting. The statements he'd made about his father were likely baseless, Ozzie told himself optimistically. He could still be alive somewhere.

Then he recalled the initials that appeared on the handkerchief Alfie had found: *SZ*. Spangler Zweig. So Tara was married now.

What sort of man would want to marry *her*? Pilar wondered. A *dicho* her mother often used told her: "*Dime con quién andas y te diré quién eres.* Tell me who walks beside you, and I will tell you who you are."

"You have some information to share," Holmes said to Pilar.

She gazed up, taking in all of Master's impressive height. Remembering his constant warnings not to put themselves in harm's way, she decided not to mention the tunnels, and instead recounted the details of their meeting with Carlos.

"And what else did this clairvoyant have to offer?"

Pilar detected some mockery in Master's voice and it irked her. "Besides rescuing us from a gang of roughs," she answered tartly, "he told us that Tara has a history of violence and attempted murder."

Holmes eyed her. Then he turned to Wiggins who reported on the creepy-looking building, its visitors, and what Alfie had witnessed in the garden. "Simpson even tracked a bloke back to Parliament."

"Holmes, imagine!" Watson exclaimed. "The affairs of state may be guided by a mere table turner."

Holmes looked at his partner with a flash in his eye. "Unfortunately, my friend, my brother, Mycroft, has confided instances where decisions have been made on information even less reliable."

Ozzie removed the handkerchief from his pocket and handed it to Holmes.

Holmes examined it thoroughly before handing it back. "What do you make of it, Osgood?"

Ozzie explained his earlier deductions. "And note the silk fabric, the initials in the German Fraktur type: It belongs to a wealthy German man, Spangler Zweig."

Holmes nodded thoughtfully, rose from his chair, and walked to his mantel. He removed tobacco from the Persian slipper, stuffed his pipe, and struck a match to light it. He stoked the pipe and disappeared into a thought.

Pilar and the boys sat on the settee and waited for him to resurface.

Just then, Billy knocked on the door and entered the flat. "Miss Elsa Hoff is here to see —"

Before he could finish, Elsa burst into the room.

Watson stood, as did Wiggins and then Ozzie. Pilar looked up at them, surprised. They had never once stood for her when she entered a room.

Elsa collapsed on a chair. Her houndstooth wool knickerbockers were coated in mud. She attempted to speak, but could only sputter through her tears.

Watson placed a hand on her shoulder to comfort her. Wiggins motioned to do the same but stopped himself. When he returned to the settee, Pilar elbowed him in the ribs.

Wiggins gave her a quizzical look.

Pilar ignored it and observed Elsa's short hair and men's clothing. Though she wanted to dislike her, she found herself riveted.

Elsa dried her eyes and dabbed her nose with a handkerchief.

Holmes observed her without a word.

"Please forgive my lack of composure, but I have never had an attempt made on my life before and I find it most disagreeable." Elsa forced a smile.

Ozzie, Wiggins, and Pilar sat up straighter and exchanged glances.

"Oh . . . my," Watson stammered and then forced a chuckle at Elsa's attempt to make a joke.

Holmes said soberly, "I appreciate your calm demeanor, Miss Hoff, and thankfully, you appear well at this time. Now if you will, pray describe what occurred."

"Shortly after I returned home, I rode my bicycle to an appointment with my aunt's solicitor, regarding my inheritance. I realize it is not entirely proper for a lady to ride a bicycle through the streets of London. But as I mentioned when we first met, my aunt raised me to think for myself, and so I travel as I wish, even though I receive disapproving comments on occasion.

"My meeting with the solicitor continued for some time. Since I know little about financial matters, I insisted that he explain everything in detail. Afterward, I decided to distribute women's suffrage pamphlets on the street where his office is located.

"For one hour, I stood in the same spot. People can be extremely rude in such situations, and today was no exception. More than one *gentleman* told me to get out of the way or called out, 'Balderdash!' I soon noticed a carriage take position just up the street from me. The driver had the most wild and unkempt appearance: a huge mane of filthy gray hair, a wiry beard that made him look less than human, and a coat with so many tears it approached shreds. He glared at me. No one entered or exited the carriage. It simply waited. After another twenty minutes, I sensed that either the driver or an unseen occupant was waiting for me. Unnerved, I started walking. I turned the corner, crossed Bond Street, and entered a milliner's shop called Adelaide's. The carriage followed me, paused momentarily, and then sped off.

"I began to think that I was in no danger and that my imagination was simply having its way with me. For a few minutes, I feigned interest in the hats in the shop. But I was still feeling a bit shaken and decided to quit distributing my pamphlets for the day.

"I had made it about halfway across the street before I realized that a horse and carriage were bearing down on me, and their master was none other than the wild man I described. I am embarrassed to say that I screamed before gathering my faculties enough to dive out of the horse's path. I surely would have been trampled if I had paused a moment longer.

"The carriage drove off frantically and turned at the next street. Some strangers helped me to my feet and assisted me into a hansom, which I took directly here. I must say, I don't know if this is related to Konstantine or to my actions on behalf of women's voting rights. In either instance, I don't like it."

Watson exclaimed, "The villains, Holmes! We must do something."

Holmes stood by the window, his pipe aloft in one hand and his eyes closed. To a casual observer, he might have appeared to be asleep, but Ozzie could tell he was visualizing the scene Elsa had just described.

When Holmes's eyelids slowly lifted, his gaze settled on Elsa. "Miss Hoff, you have once again provided an excellent account of the events that brought you here. Though I know you have had a trying day, I need you to answer a few questions."

"Certainly."

"Did you see the occupant of the carriage?"

"Through the glass, I glimpsed the outline of a male passenger, nothing more."

"Your attorney, do you trust him?"

"Yes, sir, I do. He was not only my aunt's solicitor, but her dearest friend."

"How long have you been a suffragist?"

"Two years."

"And have you ever been threatened with violence before?"

"No, sir."

Holmes reached for a match from the desk and relit his pipe. "There are those who will go to great lengths to stop such activities. How —"

Before Holmes could ask his next question, Elsa spoke.

"Oh, I have forgotten to show you something." She opened her handbag and removed an old brown envelope. "I found this amongst my aunt's personal effects earlier this morning." Elsa handed the letter to Holmes. "My uncle Gunther wrote it to my aunt many years ago. As you'll see, it begins, 'My dear little *Bisho*.'"

Holmes looked at the document with a spark in his eye. "Yes, *Bisho*. Clearly a pet name your uncle used for your aunt. It is the Xhosa word for . . ." Holmes paused. "Buffalo."

Elsa began to laugh as did Pilar and the boys. Watson flashed Holmes a quizzical look.

Holmes read the letter in full and then paced the room, stopping before the window. "A pet name of this nature would only be used between a husband and a wife. It would only appear in the most intimate of correspondences. I am sure that no other person in the world knew that your uncle referred to your aunt by this word. Where did you find this letter?"

"It was hidden in Aunt Greta's closet. In a box filled with private letters and documents."

Holmes smiled a smile that Watson and the boys recognized as confirmation of a theory.

He's likely just solved the case, Ozzie thought with excitement and a pinch of envy.

Holmes's grin broadened as he gazed out the window. And then, before anyone knew what was happening, he threw down his pipe and raced out of the flat.

Though it took them a minute to react, the boys, Pilar, and Watson followed.

Downstairs, Holmes exploded out the door of 221B Baker Street and sprinted toward a carriage manned by a driver with wild hair, a wiry gray beard, and disheveled clothes. In the passenger compartment, Ozzie spied the outline of a man in a top hat.

Upon realizing he was being pursued, the driver snapped the reins, swinging the carriage around and down the street before Holmes could apprehend him.

CHAPTER TWELVE

PILAR AND WATSON
PROTECT ELSA

You are in great danger," Holmes told Elsa back at 221B, following his unsuccessful chase of the carriage. "I am recommending that Watson return with you to your residence and remain there throughout the night."

Elsa accepted the offer. Her eyes swam with fear.

Wiggins's mind flashed back to his early days on the street, when fear was his constant companion — sleeping in dark alleys, being chased by bobbies for stealing food, the threat of being thrown in the workhouse. He had always longed for someone to take him in and keep him safe. "If you don't mind me askin', do you need another pair of eyes to assist Dr. Watson, sir?"

Pilar stared sharply at Wiggins.

Holmes glanced at him inquisitively. But before he could answer, Watson stood and said, "That's a fine idea. Pilar, why don't you accompany me and stay with Miss Hoff until she gets settled?"

"I would be happy to." She stood and curtsied, not even attempting to contain her self-satisfied grin.

Wiggins's shoulders slumped.

"Boys," Holmes said, addressing Ozzie and Wiggins, "there is still much work to be done at the mansion. I need you there."

In the parlor of Elsa's grand home, Watson reclined comfortably on a green velvet fainting couch. Pilar tried to imitate his casual demeanor, but the chair she chose felt too soft. She shifted uncomfortably and looked around.

Two crystal chandeliers hung from a ceiling painted with clouds and birds. Etched into the marble fireplace were the signs of the zodiac. Pilar located her own: Aquarius, the water bearer, before letting her gaze drift elsewhere. Landscape paintings covered the walls. Windows stretched some two stories high. Embroidered fabrics covered fancy chairs, all trimmed in whimsically carved oak. Pilar realized that her entire flat could fit into a corner of this room.

Elsa entered moments later with renewed energy and a relaxed smile. "Sorry to keep you waiting. I just arranged dinner with the cook. We shall dine at eight thirty.

"Dr. Watson, a room has been prepared for you on the second floor. Your bag is being taken up as we speak. My room is located directly above yours on the third floor. I presume you need to know that for security reasons."

"I appreciate the information, Miss Hoff. But understand, my stay here is in service to you. Please do not go to any trouble to accommodate me or my assistant here." Watson motioned to Pilar, who was still attempting to settle herself comfortably.

"Doctor, it is no trouble. This was my aunt's

home, and her full staff is still in my employ. I simply make the requests, and the work is done for me. I know there are those who think that is the same as doing the work itself. I am not so deceived." Elsa's pale eyebrows leapt playfully, a spark flickering in her green eyes.

Watson nodded with additional respect. The young woman had a thoughtful as well as a bohemian nature.

As for Pilar, she longed to be outside and wished she could go for a walk. The formality of the parlor made her legs feel restless.

Elsa seemed to read her thoughts. "I wish to change my clothes for dinner. Would you care to join me? I'm afraid this room can be a bit cold at times."

Pilar brightened and the two climbed the grand stairwell, side by side.

Moments later, they sat on the floor in a small sitting room attached to Elsa's bedroom. "Tell me about those two boys," Elsa said. "The tall, skinny lad with the bowler has such intense eyes for someone so young. He reminds me of a young Mr. Holmes."

"That's Ozzie. He's a genius. He can look at a person's handwriting and tell you all about them. He used to apprentice a scrivener who was really a forger. And he can make deductions just like Mr. Holmes.

"He's brave, too. He and Wiggins saved my life once. Ozzie's brain works at lightning speed. He becomes so lost in thought that he forgets to be scared. But he needs to take care because he has very weak lungs and tires easily. Mamá says people with sick lungs don't live long." Pilar's voice trailed off and her eyes clouded.

Elsa nodded sympathetically. "What about the other boy, the handsome one with the curls?"

"Wiggins. He's the leader of the Baker Street Irregulars. He's smart, too, but in a different way from Ozzie. He knows where to scrounge for food and how to get on with people, and he can sense whether a stranger is trouble or not. He's been on the streets since he was four and created a home for the Irregulars . . . in an abandoned building . . . I'm sorry, but I can't tell you where it is."

"You mean the boys live together? Don't they have parents or family?"

"There's a whole gang of them, twelve in all if you include Alister who's in the workhouse. Most of their parents are dead or in jail or have abandoned them. But they have one another. Ozzie thinks he has a father somewhere. He has an old aunt in Oxfordshire who might know where he lives. He's been trying to find her for months."

"What did you call them? The Baker Street Irregulars?" asked Elsa.

Pilar explained. "That's what Mr. Holmes calls them, the Baker Street Irregulars."

Pilar plucked at the purple satin lining of her cape.

"Did someone make that for you?" Elsa asked.

"Yes, my friend, Penelope . . . when Mamá and I traveled with the circus." A lump lodged in Pilar's throat. She rubbed her neck and swallowed.

"You worked in a circus?! How exotic. What did you do?"

"Mamá had a fortune-telling act. I assisted," Pilar offered somewhat hesitantly, in part because of Elsa's bad experience with Spiritualism, in part because, well . . . maybe Mamá was a fraud, too. If she could lie to her own daughter, why not to perfect strangers?

Elsa nodded thoughtfully. "Aunt Greta showed me that some people really do have the gift of clairvoyance. Do you and your mother?"

Pilar stroked the lining of her cape. "I don't know." And then for reasons she did not understand, she found herself telling Elsa the whole story of her Spanish ancestry and Mamá's fabrications about them being Gypsies. It wasn't like Pilar to dither on and on with someone she hardly knew. She had only shared a little with Ozzie and nothing at all with Wiggins.

"Does it really matter where you come from?" Elsa asked when Pilar finished. "I don't think clairvoyance has much to do with bloodlines, but more with deep intuitive powers that certain people know how to channel and others not. Look at Mr. Holmes, for example."

"Oh, no!" Pilar said. "He only believes in science. Deduction is all about science and facts." Nevertheless, Elsa's words had an effect. Maybe I do have intuitive powers, Pilar thought, even if I'm not a Gypsy.

"Yes, perhaps," Elsa agreed. "But there seems to be something else going on with that man. I think my aunt would agree." Elsa winked at Pilar.

"Well, you mustn't ever tell *him* that," Pilar said, "or he will drop your case."

They both laughed as the bell rang for dinner.

CHAPTER THIRTEEN

STRANGE HAPPENINGS
AT THE MANSION

There were flashes in the shrubbery and lightnin' bolts shootin' out of the windows!" Elliot said when Ozzie and Wiggins met him at his post in front of the mansion.

"If there is any evil involved in this case, it is made by humans," Ozzie reassured him. It was no secret that Elliot was superstitious. And Ozzie and Wiggins couldn't afford to lose him to his fears.

"I'm not afraid of no boy or man. But sprites — me da' warned me of such things. Many a good man 'as met a bad end by disturbin' those who shouldn't be disturbed." Elliot's face darkened.

Wiggins could tell he was thinking about wee Maureen. Rohan had once confided to Wiggins that Elliot said she visited him in his dreams, always in her nightie, with a laurel wreath atop her red curls.

Just then, a flock of crows screeched across the mottled sky. The boys shuddered in the darkness.

Before they could determine their next move, someone — or something — let out an unearthly howl, followed by another and another. Elliot fell backward, clutching his heart.

Wiggins looked in all directions. Then, down the street, he saw Alfie. Dragging him by a long rope was King Henry — the howler.

"Elf, I've a mind to clobber you, you *lump of school*," Elliot said when they approached.

"Oz, give me the handkerchief and we can track that bloke who disappeared. King 'Enry is ready for the job."

Wiggins grabbed Alfie by the ear. "How long 'ave you been gone from your post? What if you missed somethin' important?"

"Ow! There ain't nothin' there but a hedge, boss," Alfie said, worming free. "I want some action."

"You *sprog*. We ought to toss you and that mongrel right in the Thames," Elliot said threateningly.

King Henry growled at him.

Elliot snarled at King Henry.

"That's enough," Wiggins said. "We're goin' to stand out like old fish. Take that dog, Elf, and *lam off*."

"But —"

"Now!"

Alfie kicked a stone and scowled. "Come on, 'Enry, we'll find our own case to solve." With that, he and the dog turned back down the street.

Wiggins pulled his hair in frustration, then instructed Elliot to maintain his post while he and Ozzie checked on the others.

Simpson and Fletcher reported that they had heard strange popping sounds at the back of the mansion. Barnaby and Pete had seen flashes of colored lights coming from within. Though they made their reports calmly enough, all four seemed spooked.

As Ozzie and Wiggins crept down a small side street to find Rohan, the smell of sulfur hung in the air. "Everyone's gone *barmy*!" Wiggins said.

"We don't believe in hocus-pocus, right, mate?"

Wiggins smiled. "Right."

Just as he and Ozzie reached Rohan near the door to the tunnels, a carriage trotted noisily toward them. The three boys hid behind some empty crates and watched the coachman lift a lantern and swing it. Ozzie caught a glimpse of his face. Immediately, he recognized the wild, dirty gray hair and thick beard. Wiggins nudged Ozzie's shoulder, indicating that he had made the same connection.

After scanning the street for a minute more, the coachman knocked on the side of the carriage. Out stepped a man with a military bearing, wearing a top hat. He strode swiftly to the door that entered the tunnel, unlocked it, and waved the coachman on before slipping inside.

Once the coachman sped away, Ozzie ran to the

door, put his ear to it, and signaled to Wiggins and Rohan. "Time to try it, Wiggins."

Holmes's words echoed in Wiggins's head: "*No heroics, boys.*"

Ozzie looked at his friend hesitating in the dark. Was he respecting Master's wishes, or was he afraid? *Was* there something to fear? "We need to find out who that man was," Ozzie said.

Wiggins nodded. He could still see the look of fear in Elsa's eyes. And there was also Shirley, trapped somewhere inside the tunnels. "What about the dogs?"

"What dogs?" Rohan looked alarmed.

"If we hear them, we'll turn back," Ozzie offered. "Just a *butcher's hook*, Wiggins."

"Always know when to use the Cockney, Oz. Okay, we'll have a look." Wiggins pulled out a key, hanging on a string around his neck, and handed it to Ozzie.

"What's that?" Rohan asked.

"A skeleton key. It opens most locks. Locksmiths use it. So do thieves . . . and detectives." Ozzie put his ear to the lock as he jiggled the key.

"I did a favor for a smithy. He gave it to me," Wiggins told Rohan as the lock clicked open.

"Okay, boys," Ozzie whispered, "move as silently as . . ."

"Spirits," Wiggins finished, and the three boys entered the hidden passage.

CHAPTER FOURTEEN

A SURPRISE IN THE TUNNELS

The tunnel seemed darker and colder than the last time they'd entered. The chill air hurt Ozzie's lungs. He reached inside his coat for his tonic. Fighting back the itchy feeling of an oncoming attack, he took a swig.

Meanwhile, Wiggins pulled a box of matches from his trouser pocket and struck one. It cast just enough light to illuminate a small patch around them. Optimistically, he had hoped that Shirley would be waiting for him, front paws perked and ready for the bread crumbs he'd brought. No such luck.

"Shirley," he called softly now and again as they walked.

The dank, enclosed space unnerved Rohan, and the smell — like Elliot's dirty feet — made his stomach roil. He tried to picture himself on a Sunday adventure with his father, strolling along the banks of the Thames or watching a Punch-and-Judy show in the park. Even baiting fishhooks would be more appealing than prowling through a dark tunnel that might house vicious dogs.

Wiggins lit match after match until they had passed through the cavern and down a passageway toward the glowing doorway of the cellar.

Just then, a faint popping noise interrupted the quiet. "Did you blokes hear that?"

Ozzie and Wiggins shook their heads.

They had continued for only a minute more when an explosion or gunshot sounded in the distance. All three boys froze.

There was no telling how long they stayed that way. When all seemed quiet again, they entered the cellar, where Ozzie found a small lantern hanging from a hook on the wall. Taking the matches from

Wiggins, he lit it and walked around the room so the boys could examine everything: a narrow staircase leading to a doorway at the top of one wall, a three-foot-high platform in the center of the room, a metal tube running from the floor to the ceiling, steamer trunks, ladders, and lanterns.

The boys poked around. In one trunk, Rohan found capes, in another Ozzie discovered some sort of machine — like a large gas lamp with a long cylinder extending from its front. Wiggins opened a third trunk, reached inside, and gasped. The contents emanated an eerie light, and when he pulled out his hand, it glowed.

"Does it burn, mate?" Ozzie asked.

Wiggins shook his head disbelievingly and wiped his hand on his trousers, but the glow remained.

Ozzie motioned for Wiggins and Rohan to follow him up the narrow staircase. At the top, they opened the door and stepped into a tight passageway with paneled walls. Eventually, they arrived at a window overlooking an octagonal room, dimly lit by gaslights. A round mahogany table and chairs sat in the center.

"The séance room," Ozzie whispered.

"Why is there a window?" Rohan asked.

"It must not look like a window on the other side. Its function must be disguised in some way. Maybe it's a mirror," Ozzie reasoned. "Otherwise, the clients could see into this passageway."

Rohan lifted a large lanternlike object. Reflectors lined the inside and the cutout profile of a man had been inserted into the front. After the boys examined it, Ozzie lit it and discovered that the cutout cast a silhouette.

To the right of the window, Wiggins noticed a rope running through two pulleys. When he tugged it, the table in the center of the room began to rise.

Ozzie turned a knob at the base of the window and puffs of smoke poured into the room. "It sure looks like hocus-pocus, doesn't it, Wiggins?" The exertion up till now caused him to wheeze. He took another swig of his tonic. "Let's keep moving."

The boys continued through the tight passage-way, which ran the perimeter of the séance room, until it ended at a wall. They circled back only to dead-end at another wall.

"Look for a trapdoor," Ozzie instructed. "There must be a way into that room. I am going back down into the cellar to see if there's an entrance from there into the séance room."

"Oz . . ." Wiggins said. "I'll go."

"I am fine," Ozzie reassured him. "I will be careful."

Rohan and Wiggins felt their way back and forth through the passageway. They were slipping past the window looking in on the séance room when Ozzie sprung up, flew past their view, and landed with a thud.

Wiggins and Rohan exchanged a glance, then hurried down the passageway toward the cellar. Rohan stopped and leaned against the wall to catch his breath for a moment when, in a flash, a hidden panel gave way behind him. He yelped and landed in the séance room next to Ozzie.

Hearing the thud, Wiggins stepped through the open panel and found both boys on the floor. He offered them each a hand and grinned. "Come on, mates. We've no time to be lyin' about."

CHAPTER FIFTEEN

KONSTANTINE REVEALED

After leaving the séance room, the boys raced down a dark hallway until voices stopped them. They peered around the corner into a dimly lit library. A fire roared in the hearth. Shelves with no books climbed all the way to the sixteen-foot ceiling. Tara sat erect on a sofa arguing with a man. Though the boys could see only his back, it was clear that he must be the one they'd followed into the mansion — Spangler Zweig.

Why did he enter and exit via a secret doorway? Ozzie wondered.

"Tara, darling, every wealthy person in London with a taste for Spiritualism has come through our door in the last few months. Business has never been finer. If this continues for the rest of the year, we will never have to work again. We no longer need the girl's money." Zweig spoke confidently with only the trace of an accent.

"That money belongs to *you*," Tara countered. "I have told you for years to claim what is rightfully yours, but you haven't. Now that sad old buffalo is dead and look where it has left us."

"No reason to speak ill of the dead, my love. What you propose is too extreme. To earn the confidence of a client such as Greta, and then reap the reward is one game, but murder is quite another. Perhaps we can obtain the money by other means."

Tara shot up and stormed across the room. "No! Only when that wretched girl is gone will you acquire everything. And only then can we quit this cursed business. It is Konstantine's money as well. His birthright! If you are not willing to do away with that wretch, then I will do it myself."

Through the darkness, the boys tried to gauge one another's reactions. The "wretched girl" had to be Elsa. So someone *was* trying to kill her — and it was Tara!

Ozzie stored in his memory every detail of what was said. But he realized that one piece of the puzzle didn't add up. It kept knocking around his brain: How could Spangler Zweig be entitled to Elsa's fortune?

Zweig walked over to Tara and unfolded her arms, which were wrapped fiercely across her chest. He drew her into an embrace. "I love your strength and spirit, darling. I will finish the matter."

The fireplace provided only a dim half-light, but when Zweig turned, the boys saw a ruggedly built man in his early fifties with a neatly trimmed mustache. Something about him looked familiar to Ozzie.

As the boys watched the scene in the library, Wiggins detected a light bobbing down the hallway toward them. He tapped Ozzie's and Rohan's shoulders, signaling them to slip away.

They crept along until they entered a foyer. Then Wiggins led them up the large circular stairwell to the second floor. There they ran into an empty bedroom and gazed out a window over-looking the back garden. They realized with dismay that they were much too high up to safely lower themselves through it.

Wiggins pulled his hair. "Any suggestions?"

Ozzie pointed along the roof to another window at the far end of the mansion. It opened onto a drainpipe that led down to the garden.

Wiggins nodded. "Let's go."

They stole through the long hallway. Thankfully, all of the rooms appeared to be empty. Rohan stepped into one, thinking he could look out another window and better ascertain their posi-tion. But he was met by a low growl and then savage barking. In an instant, two lean and muscular black dogs charged him.

Rohan held his breath, leapt back into the hall-way, and slammed the door behind him.

"Those the dogs you were talkin' about, mate?" Rohan whispered, gasping for air.

The animals continued to bark ferociously.

"Maybe we should go back through the tunnels," Wiggins suggested.

Ozzie shook his head. "We can't risk returning to the ground floor." He led the boys to the room at the far end of the mansion, put his ear to the door, and cautiously opened it.

The room was dark, the shades drawn. The boys could just barely make out a four-poster bed, a wardrobe, and a washstand. They crawled toward the window that led out to the drainpipe.

Just as they were about to open the window, a blast of light exploded over their heads.

"Who bothers Konstantine's sleep?!"

The boys spun around as two loud explosions and a shower of sparks rained down, casting enough light to reveal a slim, curly-haired boy with piercing eyes.

His gaze fell upon Ozzie. "The urchin from the street! How did you get in here, you little thief? And why are you following me?"

The boys froze. Wiggins and Rohan looked to Ozzie for a plan.

"You think I'll raise the spirit of your father? Ha!" Konstantine taunted. "He would not want to visit such a worthless soul as yourself."

Rohan's eyes grew wide.

Ozzie felt suddenly light-headed. *Was* his father dead?

Before Ozzie could determine what to do, Wiggins rushed Konstantine, only to meet with another shower of sparks, which catapulted him backward against a paneled wall.

Ozzie and Rohan watched in horror as Wiggins vanished.

At the same time, urgent voices came from down the hall.

Konstantine's eyes flashed. Flames shot from his hands. "I will turn you two to ash!"

Rohan felt his legs running, lunging straight for Konstantine, a roar forming in his throat.

Konstantine hurled another flame, which sent Rohan diving for cover.

The room was now filled with smoke. The smell of sulfur made Ozzie's eyes burn and his throat constrict. He bent over coughing. That's when he noticed bits of paper and cardboard littering the floor. Konstántine's powers weren't supernatural; he'd been throwing fireworks.

Meanwhile, Rohan crouched by the washstand and rubbed his shoulder. Ozzie met his gaze and motioned to the water basin. As Konstantine wound up to launch another explosive, Rohan lifted the basin and hurled the cold water.

Konstantine let out a howl, which dwindled into whimpering sobs.

Standing there in his wet sleeping gown, he looked like a frightened child caught in a rainstorm.

Ozzie laughed. "The great Konstantine!"

Just then, a knock came at the door. "Konny, open the door at once!"

Konstantine squeaked, "Papa, help!"

"To the window, quick!" Ozzie told Rohan.

As they raced over, the four-poster bed slid across the floor and knocked Konstantine hard into the wardrobe.

Ozzie and Rohan blinked in the semidarkness.

From a hole in the floor where the bed had been, Wiggins emerged. "If you blokes are done playin' about, we may have time to *pinch* a snack in the kitchen."

Ozzie and Rohan returned his grin and followed him down the stairs at a run. As the bed slid along a small rail back over the hole, two men broke through the door.

CHAPTER SIXTEEN

THE BOYS RETURN TO 221B BAKER STREET

M r. Holmes 'as been waitin'," Billy told Ozzie, Wiggins, and Rohan when they arrived at Master's flat.

The boys could hear the music before they saw him, a slow, melancholic piece.

Master's eyes were closed, and his chin tilted inward, securing the violin to his left shoulder. His right arm drew the bow across the strings, gliding it back and forth in a delicate dance. And his body swayed with the notes, as though the music moved him, rather than his movements creating the sound. Ozzie found it hypnotic.

The music made him remember a reading Madam Estrella had once given him. "The coming year will be one of great challenges and triumphs," she'd said. "The spirits tell me that someone is watching over you. I see the figure of a man, but his face is not clear. I see puffs of small clouds . . . I see shadows . . . I hear a violin." Was it Ozzie's father that Madam Estrella had seen? Did he play the violin, too? Or was it just Mr. Holmes?

Shaking off the daydream, Ozzie focused again on Master. It was more than the music that was so mesmerizing, he realized. It was the spirit with which Master played. Ozzie had never seen him show passion for anything other than his work.

Music always made Wiggins want to sing, but the tune Master played was hard to tap your foot to. He let his gaze drift to a silver dome resting over a plate on the table. His stomach rumbled. None of them had eaten since morning.

For Rohan, the music brought back memories of his father's flute playing, and he felt a burning sensation in his chest.

As soon as Holmes opened his eyes and saw the boys, he abruptly stopped playing and placed his violin on a stack of books in the corner.

The boys clapped, causing Holmes's face to contort. Ozzie couldn't tell if it was from pride or embarrassment.

Holmes cleared his throat and said dryly, "Thank you, boys, but Sarasate has nothing to fear."

The boys had no idea who he referred to, but guessed it was a famous violinist.

Holmes stepped to the mantel and reached for his pipe. Observing Wiggins, who was still eyeing the platter hungrily, he said, "Despite Mrs. Hudson's best efforts, I am afraid I have not touched the meal she has prepared for me. Sometimes eating is a mere irritation. You boys would be improving my relations with the landlady if you consumed my dinner." He waved his hand and then struck a match.

The boys dove at the platter, then sat on the floor in front of the fire and ate cold woodcock and asparagus with their hands.

Ozzie, Wiggins, and Rohan alternated telling the story of how they witnessed Spangler Zweig exit the carriage and enter the secret passage to the mansion. In his excitement, Wiggins described the mechanisms they discovered in the cellar and the passageways. Ozzie explained the platform that shot him through the floor of the séance room.

Holmes sat in his armchair, nodded, and puffed on his pipe. In spite of their work, he didn't seem pleased. "How many times must I warn you boys not to place yourselves in harm's way. Entering the house was reckless and —"

Before he could finish, Pilar strode swiftly into the flat unannounced and handed Holmes a letter.

For once, Wiggins was grateful for her boldness and the interruption.

Holmes paused and gave Pilar a brief scowl before examining the letter. He then stood and crossed the room to the fireplace mantel.

Wiggins offered the last scrap of woodcock to Pilar as she settled herself between him and Ozzie. She shook her head. "I have had turtle soup, red mullet, and lamb cutlet, and would have had to stuff myself with more if the letter had not arrived. I've never eaten so much."

Wiggins gazed down at the small bird carcass that lay on the platter and then back at Pilar. "The ones that don't appreciate it always get the feast," he mumbled under his breath.

Pilar ignored him and looked up at Holmes. "The letter was written by a man who claims to know the circumstances surrounding Greta Berlinger's death. The author asks Elsa to meet him at the center of London Bridge on the east-side pedestrian way at ten o'clock tomorrow morning. I believe he is the same man who has been following Elsa about in the carriage, Spangler Zweig. Do you agree, Mr. Holmes?"

Rereading the letter, Holmes very nearly shook with excitement. His gaze darted from the letter to the mantel where the photograph of Gunther Berlinger sat beside the old letter he had written to Greta.

Ozzie and Wiggins recognized the gleam in Master's eyes: He had just confirmed his deductions.

Pilar seemed annoyed that Holmes was ignoring her question.

"Yes, Pilar," he said at last, his voice brimming with enthusiasm, but his eyes still not focused on her. "You are correct." Holmes placed the letter on the mantel next to the other case evidence. He clasped his hands behind his back and paced before them. "Boys, please continue with the results of your investigation."

Ozzie wanted to howl with frustration. Master had solved the mystery, he was sure, and yet he said nothing!

Ozzie squinted and studied the two letters and the photograph. The answer is there, he thought. If you think hard enough, you can decipher the case yourself. *Think*.

Meanwhile, Wiggins summarized the conversation the boys overheard between Spangler Zweig and Tara, and how Tara convinced Zweig that he must eliminate Elsa. "They are greedy, sir. They want Greta Berlinger's money and think murdering Elsa is the solution."

"That's the part I don't understand," said Rohan. "If they kill Elsa, how do they get the money? Isn't it in a bank or somethin'?"

Holmes nodded without speaking.

Wiggins went on to explain their encounter with Konstantine and their escape.

"Fireworks!" Pilar exclaimed. So her feelings about him *had* been right. Konstantine was a fraud. I can trust my intuition, she thought.

Ozzie was so entranced studying the evidence on the mantel that he hardly heard his friends talking.

Holmes returned to his armchair. "Wiggins, the fruits of your investigation are most useful and, in fact, we have all the pieces of this puzzle in part because of your work. But, as I said before Pilar interrupted . . ." Holmes paused and raised one eyebrow. "You are to use restraint and better judgment in the future."

Wiggins lowered his head. "Yes, Mr. Holmes."

"Now, pray tell me how did you follow Spangler Zweig into the tunnels? He most surely locked the door behind him." Holmes's stare was as sharp as a talon.

Ozzie stirred from his trance and looked sympathetically at his friend.

"Well, you, aah . . ." Wiggins raised a hand to the bottom of his throat.

Holmes's demeanor lightened. "Kindly remove the skeleton key from the string around your neck, my boy." He held out his hand as Wiggins complied.

"I admire your ingenuity. Many petty criminals would not know how to obtain and use such a key."

A smile spread across Wiggins's face.

"But," said Holmes, closing his fingers around it, "you boys must be more careful. Because of your station, the police could easily mistake you for common thieves, and arrest and jail you if you were ever caught using such a tool. You understand?"

The boys nodded, in part to relieve themselves of Master's scrutiny.

Pilar rolled her eyes. Master might be warning them out of protectiveness, but hadn't *he* unlawfully entered premises if a case so required? Why could adults break the rules as long as they had a reason? Mamá would not tolerate lies from Pilar under *any* circumstances, and yet she excused it in herself.

Ozzie turned back to the mantel. Studying the photograph, his face suddenly sparked with recognition.

"Osgood, have you something to say?" Holmes asked.

Ozzie sat up straighter and returned Master's gaze. "Yes, sir. I believe I can answer Rohan's question. I know how Spangler Zweig and Tara can get Elsa's money."

CHAPTER SEVENTEEN

OZZIE'S
DEDUCTIONS

Before I begin, sir, may I use your magnifying glass?"

Holmes motioned toward the desk.

Ozzie stood and retrieved it, then strode back to the mantle and lifted the letter that Pilar had just delivered. He studied the handwriting, examined the paper, and held it up to the light, which revealed the watermark.

Wiggins marveled at his friend even before he started his deductions. Other than knowing that Konstantine was a fraud and that Elsa was in danger, Wiggins could not put together the puzzle of this case. How did Ozzie do it?

Piece by piece, Ozzie examined the remaining evidence: the letter that Elsa had brought earlier that day, which Gunther had sent to Greta some twenty years prior, and the photograph of Gunther's face. Ozzie's hands shook with excitement. "I am ready, sir."

"Please," Holmes said with a puff of his pipe.

Ozzie clasped his hands behind his back and paced to the center of the room where everyone could see him. He had learned from Master that one should have fun with deductions, and a bit of theatrics amused the audience.

"First we have the séance, where Greta Berlinger died. Someone — or something — appeared as Gunther Berlinger. Was it a spirit or an actor?" He paused and let the group consider the question.

"One thing is clear," he continued, "the resemblance to Gunther was so striking that it literally frightened Greta to death."

Ozzie held out his hands, palms up. "Now, much of what we learned we overheard in conversations between Spangler Zweig and his wife, Tara. The first one Alfie described to us, the second we witnessed ourselves. Those conversations show that Zweig and Tara planned to swindle Greta of her fortune by convincing her that Konstantine could conjure Gunther. They did not *intend* to scare Greta to death, only to gain her confidence through trickery and take her money along the way.

"Greta's death created a problem. Suddenly, Zweig and Tara had lost a rich and gullible client, and now Elsa Hoff, the sole beneficiary of Greta's estate, would inherit all of Greta's money. But . . . if Elsa were dead, then clearly she couldn't inherit Greta's money. That is why Spangler Zweig and Tara are following her and trying to kill her. They have a plan that will allow Zweig to inherit Greta's money when Elsa is gone."

Ozzie paused and met Pilar's gaze. A proud grin spread across her face.

Ozzie felt his cheeks glow, but he pressed on. "At first, Zweig wanted to give up the scheme. But Tara has convinced him to go through with it for the benefit of their son, Konstantine." Ozzie lifted the letter Pilar had delivered. "This is the key, their fatal mistake." Ozzie paused, in part for effect, in part because he was so excited he needed to catch his breath.

Everyone's eyes were on him. Even Holmes seemed anxious for him to continue.

"The author of the letter asks Elsa to meet him tomorrow on London Bridge. The watermark shows that the paper comes from Bavaria. The writing suggests a person fluent in English with Dutch and German influences; the letters have interesting flourishes of an almost Continental design. But there is reluctance here, a halting style in the writing: The first letter or two of each word drags back before the rest of the letters in the word lean forward. Spangler Zweig comes from Bavaria but is fluent in English. And in spite of agreeing to his wife's wishes, he is ambivalent about killing Elsa."

Holmes nodded to confirm the logic.

"What confused me at first is exactly what Rohan asked," Ozzie said.

Rohan's face lit up. "How will Spangler Zweig get Greta's fortune?"

"Exactly. That is the real question here." Ozzie removed the photograph from the mantel and showed it to Wiggins and Rohan. "Do you recognize this man?"

They stared and squinted but no familiarity registered.

Ozzie tried to lead them along. "Picture this man sixteen years older."

The boys remained blank, but Pilar grew excited as the connection sparked. "I see now. . . ."

Ozzie nodded his congratulations then strode to the draperies and back again. "The man we have been following, Spangler Zweig, is really Gunther Berlinger, Greta's long-lost husband. It was not an actor *disguised* as her dead husband who appeared as a spirit during the séance. It was *actually* Gunther Berlinger, covered in white makeup to hide his age, and phosphorous powder to make him glow. That was the powder you found in the cellar of the mansion, Wiggins."

Wiggins looked at his hand, which had finally stopped glowing.

"That is why his appearance had such an effect on Greta," Ozzie continued. "She knew it was her husband, in the flesh. And only Gunther would have known Greta's pet name, *Bisho*."

"But how?!" Wiggins exclaimed.

Ozzie stroked his chin. "I am not sure about the how or why, other than that Gunther, for his own reasons, staged his death many years ago. What is clear is that he came to London with the sole intent of getting Greta's fortune for himself."

Holmes nodded, indicating that Ozzie should continue.

"This leads to the answer to Rohan's question: How does Spangler Zweig get Greta's money by killing Elsa? Since Greta had no family other than Elsa, Gunther alone has a legal claim to Greta's fortune. He simply has to come forward, drop his alias, identify himself as Greta's long-lost husband, and collect her money. Because Greta's fortune came from a gold mine on a ranch that once belonged to both her *and* Gunther, who could dispute him, especially with Elsa gone?"

Holmes nodded again, but kept his face expressionless.

Ozzie considered the master detective, sitting in his armchair, casually puffing his pipe. What would it take, Ozzie wondered, to truly impress him?

He hadn't realized that he'd stopped speaking until Holmes said, "Pray, Osgood, do finish."

Ozzie took a breath. "Since arriving in London, Gunther has been careful not to be seen at the mansion, thus his use of secret passages. Even if the authorities suspected that Elsa succumbed to foul play, it would be difficult to prove that Gunther had anything to do with it."

Ozzie picked up the two letters. "If there is any doubt to these conclusions, the letters reveal everything. We all know that the old letter brought by Elsa earlier today was written by Gunther twenty years ago. If you compare it to the letter Pilar delivered, it is clear they were written by the same hand. Spangler Zweig and Gunther are the same man."

Wiggins, Rohan, and Pilar sat silently in awe.

Holmes's sober expression faded into one of keen interest. "Well done, Osgood. You addressed every significant detail."

Ozzie felt his chest burn with pride. He wanted more of Master's praise, but the detective just studied him silently, a contemplative look in his eyes, as though he were trying to determine where Ozzie had come from.

Wiggins, Rohan, and Pilar still had questions, which they spouted off in near unison: "Where had Gunther been all these years?" "Why did he disappear?" "Why did he wait so long to resurface?"

Holmes turned his gaze from Ozzie and interrupted them. "Everything will become clear tomorrow. For now, I suggest you all retire for the night. Wiggins, have some of the boys continue their surveillance of the mansion until morning. I need you, Ozzie, Rohan, and one other Irregular to meet Watson at London Bridge at half-past nine in the morning — sharp. I will send a message to Watson at Miss Hoff's tonight."

Before Pilar could protest, Holmes stood and addressed her. "May I request the company of you and your mother for breakfast tomorrow, let us say half-past seven?"

Pilar brightened. "I will come. But my mother may not —"

"I need you both," Holmes said firmly. "Tell your mother I am willing to pay a small fee for her time and expertise." Then he rose and addressed the group. "It is time for me to leave the consulting chair. We must apprehend these swindlers at once!"

CHAPTER EIGHTEEN

EXCITEMENT AT LONDON BRIDGE

The granite arches of London Bridge stretched across the River Thames like two long serpents. The bridge, flanked by pedestrian walkways, ran from London on the north side of the river to Southwark on the south side, and was normally a busy thoroughfare. But on this bright, crisp autumn morning, an overturned cart had brought all the traffic on the center roadway to a halt.

Following Watson's directions earlier that morning, the boys took their positions. On the walkway halfway across the bridge, Wiggins serenaded the morning strollers as a brisk wind blew up from the river:

"Let charming Beauty's health go 'round,
In whom celestial joys are found;
And may confusion still pursue,
The senseless woman-hating crew,
And they that woman's health deny . . ."

Beside him, Ozzie leaned against the bridge's stone railing, held out his bowler, and surveyed the crowd for Elsa.

A thick crowd flowed by, heading toward Southwark. But most of the strollers were too hurried to be generous with their coins. Even Ozzie's coughing fits didn't seem to elicit much sympathy today.

Elliot stood at the end of the bridge on the Southwark side, also begging for change, and wearing a sad expression. Rohan swept rubbish from the walkway on the London side.

Meanwhile, Watson paced the full length of the bridge. Earlier, he had informed Elsa of her uncle's involvement in the case and told her that Gunther was likely the person who would meet her today.

Wiggins finished the last refrain of his song, checked Ozzie's empty bowler with a frown, and observed the clogged roadway. "It's crowded, Oz. What if we don't see Gunther pinch Elsa?"

Just then, a loud whistle came from Rohan's direction. Ozzie and Wiggins looked over and spied his mop of dark hair above the crowd. Once Rohan met their gaze, he indicated Elsa under a black bowler hat, walking toward them. At the same time, he pointed to a tall, rough-looking character in a torn overcoat, walking with a knotted-wood shillelagh. He appeared to be trailing Elsa from a slight distance. Rohan followed them.

Oblivious to both of them, Elsa kept her gaze high and continued walking.

"Gunther must have disguised himself," Wiggins whispered.

"That man is too tall and lanky to be Gunther," Ozzie noted. "But he looks menacing. I wonder what Gunther is up to "

Before Wiggins could fret too much over Elsa's fate, she strode by them. Avoiding eye contact, she made her way to the railing and stared out onto the

Thames. The rough stopped beside Ozzie and also gazed out at the water. A few yards away, Rohan resumed his sweeping.

Wiggins kept close watch on Elsa as he started a new song:

> *"I spied a comely maid,*
> *it was o'er her red and rosy cheeks*
> *the tears did trickle down,*
> *I thought she was some goddess fair . . ."*

After several minutes, Ozzie put his hand on Wiggins's shoulder and gave a sideways nod. Coming through the crowd, dressed smartly and swinging a cane, was Gunther Berlinger. Two men guarded him on either side. Both were broad as bulldogs. One had a large head, bare as a cannonball, the other a lightning bolt tattoo on his cheek.

Wiggins mumbled under his breath, "Miss Hoff, do not look up, but prepare yourself. Your uncle is approaching."

Elsa stiffened as Gunther strode casually up to her. He looked older in daylight, Ozzie observed.

The racket of the pedestrian traffic muffled their conversation, but Ozzie and Wiggins heard Elsa tell Gunther, "I don't think so," and Gunther's reply, "You do not understand."

Then Gunther grabbed Elsa by the arm. At first, she resisted. But Gunther whispered something Wiggins could not hear and she complied. The bodyguards pushed through the crowd and cleared a path in front of them.

Ozzie and Wiggins trailed as closely and inconspicuously as they could. Watson and Rohan eventually joined them, just as Gunther's bodyguards blocked their way. When Watson attempted to push by, the men seized him.

There was no time for Rohan to ponder his next move. With the speed of an angry bull, he ran headfirst into one of them, knocking him to the ground. Watson and Wiggins struggled with the other, and soon, all five bodies were wrestling in a tangled mass.

Meanwhile, Ozzie pursued Gunther and Elsa. The tall rough, who Ozzie spied out of the corner of his eye, now appeared to be following *him*.

Ozzie wove through carts and carriages, gaining on Gunther and Elsa, and at the same time, attempting to lose the rough. But the man was nearly on his heels.

Just then, deafening shrieks sailed up from the crowd as two white horses galloped up the walkway. Riding one horse and holding the reins of the other was Gunther's wild-haired carriage driver. In a panic, pedestrians leapt into the roadway or hugged the bridge's railing or were laid flat.

Gunther's driver rode up and handed him the reins to the unmanned horse. When Ozzie caught up to them, the driver uncoiled his whip and lashed it at him. Just before it struck him, he felt himself being yanked backward. When he turned, his breath caught.

Looming over him was the tall rough. His large, skeletal hands clamped down hard on his shoulders. It was all Ozzie could do to stave off a coughing fit and keep his wits about him.

"Osgood, must I always warn you about unnecessary heroics?" a voice hissed in his ear.

Master?

Ozzie grinned. And Holmes released him.

Before Holmes could scold him further, Gunther, who had been struggling with Elsa, punched her in the jaw, knocked her unconscious, and laid her across the front of his saddle. As Gunther climbed up into the saddle, Holmes charged the wild-haired man who lashed at him with the whip. Holmes held out his shillelagh and the whip wrapped around it. Then Holmes yanked it back and sent the whip flying.

By now, Gunther had turned his horse and was riding toward Southwark with his driver in tow.

Holmes and Ozzie scanned the bridge for a cart or a horse they could commandeer to chase them, but all the vehicles were lodged in traffic.

Suddenly, like a cannon, Elliot shot down the pedestrian walkway, shouting and waving his patchwork coat overhead.

Gunther managed to keep his horse from spooking and passed him, but the driver's mare brushed

Elliot and sent him spinning onto the ground. With Elsa lying limp across his saddle, Gunther and his driver rode off the bridge and out of sight.

Holmes and Ozzie threw up their arms in frustration.

CHAPTER NINETEEN

HOLMES AND OZZIE EACH FORM A PLAN

When at last they'd secured a hackney cab, Holmes, Watson, and the boys blazed through the streets.

Agitated, Holmes removed his disguise. When he spoke, it wasn't clear who he was addressing. "Miss Hoff came to me for assistance, and I virtually placed her in her uncle's hands. I underestimated Gunther Berlinger." His voice pitched into a range Ozzie had not heard before. "Fortunately, I have one more move. I only hope it is not too late."

"But Gunther is long gone. How will we know where to find them?" Wiggins's voice sounded as sore as his body.

"Gunther will likely take Elsa back to the mansion," Holmes answered tersely.

"Let's contact the Yard and storm the place." Rohan, who'd come through the brawl unharmed, surprised himself with such a suggestion.

Watson leaned back wearily on the hackney's cushions and sighed with exhaustion from the fight.

If Elliot had an opinion on the matter, he kept it to himself. He cradled his right arm and stared out the window. At the time, it did not look like much, but Ozzie realized now that Elliot had been hit by the horse with great force.

Sensing his assistants' dampened spirits, Holmes gave a rousing snap of his fingers. "I am not convinced that Scotland Yard would act with the delicacy needed at this time. Only you, my friends, can work with the required mix of alacrity and caution. Elsa Hoff's life may very well depend on it."

At this, the boys perked up and awaited further instructions.

Holmes rested his chin on the heel of his hand. Ozzie could see him growing detached as he determined their next move. He let his own thoughts drift. Slowly, an idea curled around the edges of his mind. He waited for it to crystallize.

"We shall make a two-pronged assault," Holmes said with his usual resolve. "Watson, you and the Irregulars infiltrate the mansion through the tunnels."

Watson's face showed dismay, which Holmes ignored.

"Be discreet — search for Elsa without letting your presence be known. Remember, we are dealing with dangerous and unpredictable characters."

"I have a suggestion, sir," Ozzie said.

Holmes nodded.

"I believe I know someone who may be able to provide added protection and assistance. . . ." He stopped himself from saying more. He didn't want to share his whole plan yet.

"Osgood, I rely on your judgment about these matters. Bring him along if you are certain you can trust him. For my part, I will distract the occupants of the mansion."

"How?" asked Wiggins.

Holmes smiled. "By entering through the front door, of course."

CHAPTER TWENTY

THE IRREGULARS MOUNT THEIR ATTACK

Exactly two hours later, Watson, Ozzie, Wiggins, Rohan, Elliot, and Carlos crouched in their hiding spot and watched a lavish carriage pull through the gates of Konstantine's mansion. When the footman exited and opened the door, out stepped a dark-complexioned, heavyset man with a trim mustache; an attractive woman wearing a black lace shawl and matching head scarf; and a girl, similarly attired, who resembled her.

Wiggins pulled out his spyglass and examined their faces. "It's them."

Watson said, "Let's proceed."

Alfie will be sorry to miss this, Wiggins thought. Since being sent off yesterday, the lad had been utterly depressed, and this morning, he had left the Castle without eating breakfast. I'll make it up to him with a feast tonight, Wiggins told himself as he, Ozzie, Rohan, and Elliot led Watson and Carlos to the entrance of the tunnels.

Gazing at the scar across Carlos's throat, Ozzie felt proud of his plan and was glad Carlos had agreed.

"I haven't always been the upstanding gent you see before you now. I've done some bad things in my life," he'd told Ozzie when he'd requested his help earlier that morning. "Maybe this will balance things."

They arrived at the side street across from the tunnel door, only to find a wild-haired figure blocking the doorway. Wiggins noticed a brougham parked a few buildings down and motioned to the others to step back into a side alley. "It's Gunther's carriage driver," Wiggins whispered with a groan.

"I have an idea," Ozzie said. "Elliot, come with me."

*   *   *

A solemn, stocky man greeted the guests in the grand foyer of the mansion. "Your Excellency, *Señor* Ambassador. *Señora* and *Señorita,* I am Christopher Brown, Konstantine's custodian." He bowed to each of them.

"The ambassador expected to be met by Konstantine himself. And you shall address me as Madam Ambassador," the woman informed Christopher with a perfunctory nod.

"Papá, these people have no sense of respect or propriety," their daughter added. "Perhaps we should find another medium to contact Juan Philipe."

"We, ah, mean no disrespect, sir. It is just our custom to —"

The ambassador dismissed the feeble apology with a wave of his hand. "Enough. I do not care for such formalities. I wish to see this Konstantine, *pronto.* Now!"

Christopher bowed awkwardly. "Indeed, sir. Follow me."

* * *

Gunther's driver looked up as his horse trotted toward him with the brougham in tow. "Blimey," he cursed. "I swear I secured the brake lever." Gazing down the street and back over his shoulder, he walked toward the carriage. The horse now trotted faster, the wheels of the brougham grinding on the cobblestones. "Princess!" he yelled. Then, upon seeing the reins moving without a driver to pull back on them, he ran faster and waved his arms in the air. "Princess?" But the horse galloped straight at him and knocked him down.

From under a blanket, Elliot emerged on the driver's seat. Snapping the reins, he cackled, "How do you like bein' laid out by your own horse, you *wally*!"

The driver groaned and pulled himself to his feet. Hobbling after the carriage and spewing curses, he didn't even notice Wiggins, Watson, Carlos, and Rohan crouching in the shadows.

"Nice trick," Carlos told Ozzie when he returned to the secret entrance.

"Elliot's dangerous when you make him angry," Ozzie said. He turned toward Rohan, who had lifted a lantern from the ground. It had a cover that slid over the lens to darken it. "Looks like our wild-haired friend left us a blackout lantern," he said.

Wiggins turned the knob, but the door to the tunnels was locked. "What rotten luck. Now what?"

Watson fished in his pocket and removed the skeleton key. "Holmes said we might need this."

Sensing that Watson hadn't a clue how to use it, Ozzie took the key. Then, with the ease of a seasoned criminal, he knelt down, slipped it in the keyhole, and turned it until the lock clicked open.

Tara welcomed the Spanish ambassador and his family into the parlor with a curtsy. She wore a fitted black dress that accentuated her slim frame, and her hair was tied back in a severe chignon. Motioning to the table and chairs in the center of the séance room, she said, "Please make yourselves comfortable."

The three guests sat.

Tara took her seat, as well. "I have traveled to *España*. I find your country quite beaut —"

"*Señora*, I would appreciate being spared your *charla*. We've no time for idle chatter. We have come to see Konstantine and are eager to contact our son." From inside his jacket, the ambassador pulled a leather sack and set it on the table. "More than two hundred pounds in gold. It is a trifle. If Konstantine has true powers and can reunite us with our beloved Juan Philipe, there will be a far greater reward."

The ambassador's wife began to weep. Her daughter glanced at her, and tears sprung to her own eyes.

Tara's gaze seized upon the sack. She cleared her throat and motioned to Christopher. "What are you waiting for? Summon Konstantine at once!"

The blackout lantern cast a wide beam, like the light from a train engine. Wiggins led Watson, Ozzie, Rohan, and Carlos into the tunnel. Periodically, he darkened the lantern so they could stand and listen. All was silent.

When they arrived at the center of the main cavern, Wiggins indicated that they should begin looking for Elsa — until he heard the padding of feet on the dirt floor, accompanied by a series of low growls.

In an instant, the two dogs, teeth gnashing, lunged at Wiggins. The lantern crashed. Wiggins cried out. Ozzie raced over, lifted the lantern, and used it to whack one of the dogs on the snout. It yelped and released its grasp on Wiggins's leg.

Rohan attempted to pull the other dog off Wiggins by its hindquarters, but it swung around and bit his arm.

By now, the dog Ozzie had hit recovered and sprung at him. But Carlos interceded, grabbing the dog by the scruff of its neck. He locked his other arm around the dog's midsection and clamped down in a vicelike grip. The dog flailed its head and snapped at the air.

Following Carlos's lead, Watson grabbed the collar of the dog biting Rohan and rapped on its snout until the boy was freed from its jaws.

"What do we do with these beasts?" Watson struggled to lock the dog in the same hold Carlos maintained. "I have never seen anything quite like them, like oversized terriers but lean and strong as Rottweilers."

Rohan rubbed his arm and slid up his coat sleeve to examine the bite. Fortunately, the skin had not been broken. "We could take 'em back down the tunnel and let 'em out on the street. But then they might attack innocent people." He frowned at the thought.

"The manacles! We can chain 'em up by the collars." Wiggins pointed down one of the tunnels. He had a patch of blood on the upper thigh of his right trouser leg, and his right sleeve had been torn clear off, revealing a long gash.

Ozzie helped Wiggins to his feet and held up the lantern to light the way. Wiggins limped alongside him.

Behind them, Watson and Carlos struggled to keep the dogs calm and quiet. "Easy, my sweets," Carlos crooned, "don't get excited now."

Watson groaned.

Konstantine entered the room in a flowing red velvet robe.

"Your Excellency, allow me to present the world-renowned medium, Konstantine." Christopher made a grand gesture toward the boy.

The ambassador nodded.

Konstantine bowed, full of self-importance. With a sweep of his robe, he sat as Christopher dimmed the oil lamps and then departed.

"*Perdóname*. Pardon me, but I would like to ask a question," the ambassador's daughter interrupted.

Tara forced a smile. "I am sure Konstantine would be most obliged to answer your question."

"Will you actually produce my brother or just his voice?" she asked.

"I will try to summon your brother in bodily form, but it may require more than one visit." His eyes shined with confidence.

"Why?"

Konstantine flashed a look at his mother.

"Sometimes spirits are reluctant. Raising the dead is not like inviting someone to tea."

"¡*Cielos!* Heavens!" the ambassador's wife exclaimed. "We are all well aware of that." Then, turning to the ambassador, she added, "Your Excellency, have these people no manners?"

The ambassador reached for the leather money sack lying on the table.

"Wait!" Tara almost shrieked. "I mean . . . forgive him, us. Let us proceed."

"Very well," the ambassador's daughter said in a challenging voice. "I think my brother would like to see me now."

"Where are the manacles?" Wiggins said when they reached the end of the tunnel. "There were chains and manacles here yesterday, hanging from the wall."

"This is ridiculous," Watson said with some heat. "We stand here prisoners to these dogs when we need to find Miss Hoff and assist Holmes." At that, the dog Watson was holding growled and thrashed about.

Carlos sighed. "You cannot blame the dog for the influence of its master."

Ozzie aimed the lantern up at the wall before them. It seemed cleaner and more refined than the other walls. Standing back, he spied an empty torch sconce, which shined as if new. When Ozzie pulled it, the wall rotated, exposing a small alcove. A muffled moan, like that of a distressed animal, leaked out.

And then they saw her.

CHAPTER TWENTY-ONE

THE CONS ARE EXPOSED

As the wall rotated, Elsa — in chains — was dragged along with it. Her calls for help were stifled by a gag.

Wiggins hobbled over. Just as he started to remove the gag, his hand brushed something furry near Elsa's coat pocket. He startled. The furry thing poked its head out, jumped into his arms, and suddenly Wiggins thought *he* might scream. "Shirley!"

The ferret nuzzled under his chin. Wiggins stroked her soft fur. "You're all right, girl. You were protectin' the lady."

While the two enjoyed their reunion, Ozzie stepped around them and removed the gag from Elsa's mouth.

Elsa rubbed her jaw and stifled a cry. "I don't know how you found me. I was certain they would leave me here to die." She looked at Wiggins. "You know that creature? It's been burrowing into my pocket. Nearly frightened me out of my wits."

"Shirley's as fine a friend as you'll ever find," Wiggins reassured her. "She was keepin' you company, and watchin' over you on top of it."

Elsa managed a smile.

Meanwhile, the wall had continued to turn. Just before the compartment behind it sealed itself again, Carlos heaved his dog in and aided Watson to do the same. The animals howled for a minute until the wall revolved and closed completely. Then there was silence.

"We're happy to be of service to you, Miss Hoff," Watson said as if he had single-handedly rescued her.

Ozzie rolled his eyes and examined the locks on Elsa's shackles. "They are too small for the skeleton key. What now, Wiggins?"

Wiggins shook his head.

Carlos removed a small wire from inside his pocket and twisted it. "Excuse me, miss, may I see your wrist?"

Elsa held up the manacles.

Carlos gave the wire another turn, then inserted it into the keyhole, and jiggled. The first lock opened. Carlos removed the manacle from Elsa's left wrist, then set to work on the right.

Wiggins, Ozzie, and Rohan looked at one another, impressed.

"I have held many occupations, boys," Carlos told them. "Even the bad ones have given me useful skills."

"Thank you," Elsa said, rubbing her wrists when both were free.

Carlos took one of her hands in his and helped her to her feet. "My pleasure. And now," he said with a grin, "I believe Ozzie has an idea for a bit of fun."

The ambassador and his family, Tara, and Konstantine sat around the table holding hands.

The crystal ball glowed a bright green. As Konstantine chanted, quills of light emanated from it. A guitar across the room floated four feet off the ground and played a flamenco tune.

The seekers watched, listened, and waited eagerly.

When they reached the end of the tunnel, Ozzie and the others stopped in front of the doorway that led to the cellar. Ozzie dimmed the lantern and pointed down the hall.

From their hidden vantage point, they witnessed Christopher maneuvering a huge lantern. It projected a green beam onto an angled mirror. The beam shot up into the tube that disappeared into the ceiling. Christopher then placed a mirrored ball on the front of the lantern, spun it, and removed a green filter from the lens. Specks of white light twirled around the room and reflected off the mirror.

Watson wasted no time. "If you would kindly step up against the wall, Mr. Brown. The show is over."

Christopher startled at the sight of him. He set down the mechanism as if to comply. But then he crouched and was about to lunge at Watson when he stopped suddenly and clutched his heart. The color drained from his face, and his body shook. "I-I-I-I-I th-thought you were d-d-d-d-ead."

Carlos lifted his chin to expose the scar running across the front of his neck. "You and your sister do nice work, Chrissy, but not thorough enough. Now sit on the floor like a good chap before I start to entertain nasty thoughts about revenge."

Christopher promptly obeyed.

Wiggins pointed up the stairs to the passageway that circled the séance room. "Who is up there?"

When Christopher didn't answer, Ozzie said, "It must be Gunther."

Carlos found some rope coiled in the corner of the room. Tying it in knots, he walked over to Christopher. "These boys were talking to you, Chrissy, and they're friends of mine." He pulled the rope taut between his hands. "You had best listen to them. Now, the other gent up there, is it Gunther?"

Christopher nodded as Carlos tied him up.

"Very well, then. How shall we proceed?" Carlos asked.

Watson cleared his throat, but before he could answer, Ozzie said, "Follow me."

In the séance room, the crystal ball grew dark. Konstantine stopped chanting. His guests looked at him, perplexed.

Tara stiffened.

Konstantine collected himself and continued chanting, but the crystal remained lifeless.

"Where is my brother?" the ambassador's daughter asked in a shrill tone. "I want to see my brother! You lied to us!"

Her mother's eyes welled up as she placed a consoling hand on her daughter's shoulder. "*Lo siento, hija.* I am sorry." The two held each other and wept.

Just then, a light shined through the mirror on the wall, and the profile of a young man reflected upon it. Voices echoed in the room in response to Konstantine's chant. Tara relaxed.

But just as swiftly as it had appeared, the light behind the mirror went dark. The profile disappeared. A loud scratching sound replaced the chanting voices. And a rumbling came from behind the walls.

The ambassador cast his eyes upon Tara and Konstantine, who, in turn, darted theirs around the room.

"Spirits, I am trying to reach the son of this esteemed gentleman," Konstantine intoned, but this time with a noticeable quaver in his voice. "O spirits, speak to me!"

In a flash of smoke, a figure appeared, glowing a brilliant green.

Tara looked up, then stood and backed away. The green figure strode toward her, arms outstretched. "I have come for you, mistress, for you have wronged me!"

Tara shrieked.

Konstantine watched his mother, confounded.

Carlos paced toward her and backed her into the wall.

With terror in her eyes, Tara pulled a knife from inside her dress and brandished it. But her hands shook so violently that it dropped to the floor.

In that moment, Gunther exited a panel in the wall and fled across the room. Rohan, Watson, and Wiggins gave chase.

Konstantine rushed to his mother's aid just as Ozzie and Elsa shot up through the floor in front of him.

Ozzie saw the Spanish ambassador pursue Gunther. The ambassador's wife and daughter approached Konstantine from behind. They removed their head scarves.

When Konstantine turned to face them, he said, "Who are you?"

Unbeknownst to anyone, a small figure stood outside the mansion, waiting a few feet from the front door. As Gunther flew through it, the figu-

instructed, "Now's your moment. Be a good boy and catch 'im!"

Like a hungry beast pouncing on leftover sausages, King Henry sprung on Gunther. The leonine dog tackled him, pinned him to the ground, and clamped his jaw down firmly on the man's shoulder. By the time Watson, Rohan, Wiggins, and the Spanish ambassador flew out the door, Gunther's cries pierced the quiet night air.

"Good dog," Alfie praised, standing beside his hound and grinning.

CHAPTER TWENTY-TWO

THE CASE CLOSES

With the curtains in the library parted, light poured in, revealing a room more worn than the boys remembered. The furniture upholstery was faded, the wallpaper peeling, the floorboards badly scratched. The Irregulars and King Henry reclined on the floor, watching Carlos perform card tricks while Holmes, having removed his ambassador's disguise, spoke with Inspector Lestrade of Scotland Yard.

Elsa, Watson, Pilar, and Madam Estrella sat on a couch together, observing as, across the room, Gunther, Tara, Christopher, and Konstantine were handcuffed by police officers. Pilar and her mother, still in disguise, exchanged a meaningful glance.

After the events on London Bridge, Holmes had sent a telegram to Inspector Lestrade, who arranged for some men to stand by at the mansion. Once Gunther had been brought down by King Henry, and Carlos had Tara under control, Ozzie, at Holmes's request, summoned the officers.

Now, having finished his discussion with Lestrade, Holmes walked to the center of the room and addressed Gunther. "We know everything about your operation and your plans for Miss Hoff. Only one question remains unanswered: Why did you leave Greta Berlinger so long ago? Was it for her?" Holmes motioned to Tara, who swore and struggled against the officers holding her.

"Why are we being held?!" she shrieked. "We didn't try to kill that old cow."

Gunther looked at her. "Darling," he whispered, "calm yourself. I'll take care of everything." Then, turning to face Holmes, he said, "My love possesses a fiery passion and a temper to match. But neither of us would ever have harmed Miss Hoff."

Carlos let out a hearty laugh. "You must be

referring to another woman, sir, for that one," he pointed to Tara, "slit my throat for a pittance."

Gunther coughed as if to dismiss the accusation. "Sixteen years ago, I had business in Pretoria. A business associate and I were dining in the hotel restaurant one evening when my eyes beheld the most beautiful creature.

"My associate was acquainted with Tara Brown through her work as a medium and arranged an introduction. I was charmed to discover that her spirit matched her appearance. I had been a wild young man, and Greta provided a respectable way to settle down. But when I met Tara, I knew I had found my true love.

"I decided to leave Greta but wanted to cause her as little harm as possible. So I staged my drowning on a hunting trip. I had done well financially, and I knew she would be cared for in the manner to which she was accustomed. At the same time, I also maintained accounts that were unknown to Greta. That money would help provide for my new family.

"Tara and I left South Africa with her brother, Christopher, and relocated to Bavaria, where I assumed the identity of Spangler Zweig. We lived a fine life. Tara and I had a child together and lived happily for more than a decade. Then, some of my investments went bad.

"I had learned of Greta's newfound wealth as a result of discovering gold on our ranch, but I did not intend to bother her. To bring in money, Tara and Christopher began to perform their old medium routine, with some new flourishes that I suggested. We soon realized that our son, Konstantine, had a natural theatrical gift and eventually we made him the centerpiece of the act. You can imagine my surprise some months ago when we received a correspondence from Greta, asking to see Konstantine! About this same time, the authorities in Bavaria were causing trouble for us, so we decided to relocate to England. After being in London for a short period, we arranged, through a series of clients, for Greta to be introduced to Konstantine. I believe you know the rest." Gunther looked over at Elsa. "We never intended Greta any harm. We merely sought some of the money that was rightfully mine."

"You may not have intended Mrs. Berlinger's death," Holmes replied, "but you are guilty of swindling her and many others, as well as abducting and attempting to murder Miss Hoff. The courts will decide whether you are responsible for more."

"What about my son?" Gunther asked.

For the first time, Konstantine looked truly frightened.

"The courts will determine his fate, as well," Holmes replied matter-of-factly.

At that, Tara flailed about and tried to bite the officer holding her.

"Enough," Lestrade announced. "Take these scoundrels out of here."

After the room had cleared, Elsa said, "I must thank you, Mr. Holmes — all of you, actually. I am certain I would not have survived this ordeal without you." She smiled at Wiggins, who bowed.

Holmes gave the boys a nod of acknowledgment.

Ozzie waited for the praise he hoped would follow, but none came.

Instead, Holmes strode over to Madam Estrella and Pilar. "Thank you. Your performances as Spanish aristocrats were worthy of the West End."

Madam Estrella curtsied. Pilar beamed. Maybe there was hope for Master after all, she thought.

Wiggins looked at Ozzie and shrugged. Holmes's aloofness and inconsistency with praise were frustrating at times, but Wiggins was accustomed to it. Ozzie knew this was just Master's nature, so why did he look so disappointed? Wiggins wondered.

Before Holmes could say anything more, Alfie interrupted. "What about King 'Enry? Gunther would have gotten away if not for 'im."

King Henry seemed to understand that his curtain call had come, and he stood.

Holmes smirked and approached the dog. "But of course. King Henry, you have proven yourself to be a fine hunter." Holmes gave the dog a congratulatory pat and observed him more closely. Then he turned and addressed Alfie. "Little one, it seems you will have to change this fine beast's name."

Alfie and the others gave Holmes a puzzled look.

Without warning, Holmes broke into a hearty chuckle, the queerest sound they'd ever heard come from him. "Indeed, the king is most definitely a queen."

The boys laughed, too.

"You mean 'Enry's a girl?" Alfie asked with a mix of surprise and disappointment.

Wiggins laughed. "I guess that makes her the first girl in the gang."

Pilar shot him a look.

Holmes nodded as he inspected the dog's markings. "Tell me, boy, where did you find her?"

"He . . . er . . . I mean she was abandoned down by the Thames. Folks there say she belonged to an old mudlarker who drowned."

"That's doubtful," Holmes said. "This dog is a Newfoundland, a crossbreed of the Great Pyrenees and the boarhound. Judging by the brown speckles on her tongue, she may have another breed or two mixed into her lineage." At that, the dog attempted to give Holmes a slobbery kiss. He quickly backed away.

"Newfoundlands are excellent swimmers," Holmes continued. "They have a history of rescuing human beings from drowning. Surely such a loyal breed would never let its master drown. This fine specimen was more likely at the Thames on patrol for sinking ships. If I'm not mistaken, the police employ a hound just like this for such work."

Alfie looked crestfallen. "Does that mean we can't keep 'er?"

Holmes gave Alfie a sympathetic smile. "It means we must try to find her rightful owner. But that search can wait until tomorrow."

Alfie patted King Henry's head. She, in turn, nestled her big head onto his lap and panted.

CHAPTER TWENTY-THREE

OZZIE'S FAREWELL

The following day, Pilar and the gang gathered around the fire pit in the Castle. With the shillings Master had paid them (plus the guinea Alfie had received for finding Gunther's handkerchief), Wiggins had prepared a generous lunch of pheasant and roasted potatoes. But no one was very hungry.

"I can't believe you're leavin' us, Oz," Alfie said as he patted Queen Elsa (formerly King Henry).

"Will you come back after you find your father?" Rohan asked.

"Would *you*, if you found your da'?" Elliot said.

Rohan knew the answer and suddenly felt daft

for asking. He changed the subject. "Remember the time at the circus, Oz, when you froze climbin' up to the tightrope? You were huggin' that pole so fierce, we thought you'd never make it down."

"I am goin' to miss the stories you read us," Alfie added. "One of us blokes is goin' to 'ave to learn to read."

Ozzie raised a hand in protest. "Please don't get sentimental on me now." He had packed his satchel with some food, a blanket, the picture of his mother, and an old *Strand Magazine* that recounted one of Master's adventures. Throughout his pockets and other parts of his body (including his socks and hat), he had scattered his entire savings. A new map was tucked in his coat pocket.

Pilar and Wiggins tried to think of something to say, but couldn't.

Ozzie filled the awkward silence. "I plan to take the train from Paddington to Banbury. That is where my people are from, and I will begin my search there. If Great-aunt Agatha is alive, I will find her. She'll know something about my father, don't you think? She must have some sort of clue."

No one knew what to say.

Finally, Pilar spoke. "I worry that if she knows nothing about your father, it will be too disappointing for you. You shouldn't excite yourself, Ozzie. It's not good for your lungs." She didn't even try to disguise the concern in her voice.

Ozzie nodded thoughtfully. "If Great-aunt Agatha knows nothing, at least I can have a visit with my last-known relative."

"But if she knows something," Wiggins said softly, "you'll be gone for good."

Ozzie looked at his friend. "Even if she does and I someday find my father, I will come back to visit, I promise. And who knows, there's no saying he will want me. When my mother was still alive, he never tried to locate me. But whatever happens, I need to go on this quest." Ozzie put a hand on Wiggins's shoulder. "You understand, don't you, mate?"

Wiggins nodded. He knew that if he stood in Ozzie's shoes, he would make the same choice.

Pilar gave him a hug. For the first time, he didn't resist.

Then Ozzie waved farewell to the boys. "It's been an honor working with you all."

One by one, the Irregulars walked over to Ozzie and clapped him on the back or shook his hand. Elliot gave him a soft punch in the arm. "May the wind be at your back, mate."

Ozzie felt his throat grow tight.

Wiggins tried to lighten the mood — as much for himself as for the others. With the same cheerful assurance he brought to his performances on the street, he faced the solemn gang of boys. "Mates, we know that Oz is a city fella. There's only one great city in this land and we live in it. He'll be back, you'll see. Besides, he'll miss workin' for Master."

With that, Ozzie picked up his valise and headed toward the trapdoor. "Remember, mates," he said, turning back one last time to face them. "Nothing new or important happens without first having an adventure. We are lucky that way. Every day is new for us. Every day is an adventure."

FACTS and PRACTICALS
— for the —
ASPIRING DETECTIVE

—— SLANG GLOSSARY ——

Groat: money (page 7)

To get up your nose: to make you angry (page 8)

Daft: stupid (page 8)

Frog a log: dog (page 15)

Glad rags: good clothes (page 55)

Sprog: small child (pages 62, 105)

Collywobbles: creeps (page 71)

All mouth and no trousers: all talk and no action (page 78)

Nobs: upper class people (page 78)

Poxy: inferior (page 78)

Bonny: pretty (page 79)

Bloke: male (page 80)

Lump of school: fool (page 104)

Lam off: leave (page 105)

Barmy: crazy (page 106)

Butcher's hook: look (page 107)

Pinch: steal (page 122)

Wally: idiot (page 156)

THE ART OF DISGUISE

MAKEUP

The detective must be something of a chameleon, able to change his or her appearance in order to impersonate a wide variety of characters. Essential to the art of disguise is makeup. Note that in the story you have just read, Sherlock Holmes, with a few simple techniques, is able to transform his pale, gaunt face into that of mustached, full-faced Spanish diplomat. With the proper tools and a bit of practice, you will be able to do the same.

Some key facial alterations to consider are:

Prosthetics (fake noses, ears, and chins): For enlarging any of these parts, use a soft, moldable

putty. Take care in securing it to the areas arou
the feature you are altering, making sure there i.
no seam where it has been attached. Putty is more
convincing than a store-bought prosthetic, which
almost never creates an exact replica. Putty can
also be used to make moles, warts, welts, pimples,
and other skin blemishes. Depending on the blem-
ish, a cosmetic tint may need to be added.

Facial Hair (mustaches, beards, chin and cheek
stubble, eyebrows, stray hairs, ear and nose hair):
The trick here is finding suitable hair with the
right color and texture. Save clippings from hair-
cuts and ask friends and family members to donate
theirs to your makeup box. Remember that it is
essential to keep the attaching glue or tape invisible. To simulate hair stubble, charcoal can be
effective.

Skin Color: To darken or lighten the skin, rouges
and powders may be applied, rouges for darkening,
powders (pressed or talcum) for lightening. It's a
good idea to collect a wide range of shades. The

plication can be done with fingers, makeup brushes, and sponges. Ladies often have a good supply of these products, so you might ask your mother or sister for some. The cosmetics and applicators can also be purchased at any quality apothecary. Be sure to avoid face paint, which tends to look garish and more like a costume than a proper disguise.

Face Shape: Rouges and powders work well to fatten or slim the face. To enlarge, "paint" rosy circles sparingly on the cheeks. To thin, apply rouge in long strokes just beneath the cheekbones.

Age Creases and Scars: To simulate the age lines of an older or more weathered person, use a light brown or light gray eye-lining pencil and follow the natural creases on your own face (smile lines sloping downward from the outer edges of the nose to outer edges of the lips, "crow's feet" at the outside corners of the eyes, squint lines between the eyebrows, and worry lines on the forehead). Scars can also be drawn with a lining pencil. Choose a reddish pink color to simulate fleshy scar tissue. For truly impressive scars, use putty (tinted reddish pink) to create a raised effect.

Makeup Case: A shoe box or cigar box are fine choices for a detective's makeup case. However, fishing boxes with sliding trays are fancier alternatives. Note that something with a small handle can be useful for traveling and a good latch is helpful to avoid spillage and breakage.

Most important of all, when assuming the role of another person, believe in yourself. If you don't, surely others will not believe in you. And remember: Be clever, be thoughtful, and be convincing!

── MEDIUM CON ARTISTS ──

ny aspiring detective worth his deerstalker studies accounts of crime stories in the news. Through such study, detectives learn the patterns and characteristics of particular types of crimes, which aids them in solving future mysteries. As Sherlock Holmes advised, "Shut yourself up for three months and read the annals of crime. Everything comes in circles — even Professor Moriarty . . . The old wheel turns, and the same spoke comes up. It's all been done before, and will be again."

Accordingly, the following are classic bits of supernatural fraud, spiritual swindling, and medium con-artistry for your education and entertainment.

Madam Zingara: A medium and crystal-ball reader, Zingara learned the deep dark secrets of her clients and then blackmailed them. During a reading, she would cleverly question a client and extract embarrassing and compromising information, then threaten to expose the client, his or her family, and others if she was not paid a handsome fee.

Edgar Zug and Mrs. Sarah McBride: This Spiritualist couple dressed in black robes and defrauded clients during séances by telling them that they were cursed. They threatened the clients, saying they would suffer painful and gory deaths at the talons of evil spirits and that their only chance for survival was payment to make the demons go away. People actually gave Zug and McBride their life savings to lift the curses.

Florence Cook: This medium was said to have the power to summon and materialize the spirit of Katie King, the alleged daughter of the famous pirate, Captain Morgan. Florence Cook would disappear into a spirit cabinet (a piece of furniture similar to a wardrobe or a piece of cloth hanging in a corner of a room), and after a few incantations, the "spirit" of Katie King would appear in flowing robes. Guests were asked not to touch her for fear they would offend the spirit.

Both Cook and the woman who played King's spirit were attractive and young and received much attention (and compensation) for their work. In fact, their act received such notoriety that it captured the imagination of the famous Victorian scientist Sir William Crookes. Crookes claimed to have investigated Cook fully and vouched for the authenticity of her powers. Some say that Crookes had been duped. Others say he had fallen in love with Florence Cook or the woman who played Katie King. Photographs still exist showing the "apparition" of Katie King with Florence Cook the medium. People now believe they were really sisters.

WHAT DETECTIVES AND OTHER CITIZENS ATE

Delectable fare from sea, air, and land comprised the diet of late Victorian England.

Wealthy Victorians indulged in large, lengthy meals. It was not unusual for a dinner to have seven courses with three to five choices per course. Such a meal might include courses of soup, fish, fowl, entrée (the main course), game, sweets (a cold dessert course), and dessert.

Victorian cuisine also boasted an international flavor, particularly with the influence of Indian and French foods. Curries were common, and fancy meals often included a French dish as an entrée choice.

Imagine a side dish of sea turtle fins and guts

in sauce, or the classic pigeon pie, made from a menagerie of rump steak, pigeon, ham, butter, and eggs in a pastry shell. Or the delightful array of fowl: common birds such as chicken and duck, but also woodcock, pheasant, partridge, and grouse. And there were oysters: raw, stewed, or stuffed into pies. In fact, oysters were so plentiful they were considered a dish for the poor.

And, let us not forget the puddings! These were slow-cooked delicacies: grains or legumes wrapped in a cloth bag with spices and cooked in boiling water or hung in pots with boiling meats. Savory puddings — Yorkshire, oat, and pease, to name a few — were served as side dishes to an entrée. Sweet puddings — rice and Manchester — were served as dessert.

Good recipes for all of these dishes, save for perhaps the sea turtle fins, can still be found. Enjoy!

ACKNOWLEDGMENTS

Our deepest thanks to our agent and dear friend, Gail Hochman; our wonderful editor, Lisa Sandell; her assistant, Jody Corbett; art director, Steve Scott; Anne and Alex Dunn, readers extraordinaire; fact-checker, Deirdre David, Professor Emerita of English, Temple University; and Ellie Berger, for her support in countless ways.

Thanks also to our friends and family for putting up with our disappearances, and to Ruby and Levi, the magic in our every day.

ABOUT THE AUTHORS

TRACY MACK is the author of two celebrated novels: *Birdland*, a Book Sense Top Ten Book, a Sydney Taylor Award Honor Book, and an ALA Best Book for Young Adults, and *Drawing Lessons*, a *Booklist* Top Ten First Novel and a *Teen People* NEXT Award Finalist.

MICHAEL CITRIN is an attorney and has been a Sherlock Holmes fan since he was a young boy.

Together, Tracy Mack and Michael Citrin are the authors of the first book in the Sherlock Holmes and the Baker Street Irregulars series, *The Fall of the Amazing Zalindas*, an Agatha Award finalist. They are married and live in western Massachusetts, with their two children.